The DECEIT of a DEVIL

The
DECEIT
of a
DEVIL

HOLLY RENEE

FOR BRANDI

Since you're the one who has to deal with Carson every day.

I'm sorry this duet didn't help with his ego.

CHAPTER 1
ALLIE

I walked through the gate and grimaced when I saw Mr. Sneed waiting on me.

I was late, and I was one hundred percent sure that he noticed. Not only was I late, but I also hadn't shown up for the last week and a half. According to my mother, he wasn't very happy about it, but at this point, I really didn't have the energy to care.

"It's nice to see you show up." Mr. Sneed crossed his arms where he leaned against the porch. It looked like Carson had done quite a bit of work while I wasn't here.

I shrugged and looked around before tucking my hair behind my ear. "I wasn't feeling very good."

"Your friend said it was his fault." He nodded over his shoulder, and I knew that he was referring to Carson. He was here, and he was the absolute last person I wanted to see. "He's been working double to make up for you not being here."

"What a hero," I answered sarcastically, shocking Mr. Sneed.

"Are you two fighting?" He cocked his head to the side.

"Nope." I looked around the yard and tried to find something to do that would keep me as far away from Carson as possible. "We're exactly how we've always been."

It wasn't a complete lie. Everything I thought I had become with Carson was nothing but a lie. It was nothing but a damn game.

What we were was exactly what he had made us.

Enemies.

We had been that for a long time, but I had always hoped... I had wished things were different.

All that naivety was gone now.

I knew that we would never be anything more than exactly what we were, and I shouldn't have been angry about it.

But I was.

I was beyond angry and hurt, and I hated that I had given him the opportunity to make me either of those things. Carson was only able to hurt me because I cared about him when I shouldn't have. I cared about him, and I was even stupid enough to think that I might have loved him.

That seemed like nothing but a joke now.

"Okay." Mr. Sneed stood and his keys jangled in his hand. "I'm going to leave you two to it then. Carson's working on scraping off the peeling paint in the dining room now. He'll show you what he's been up to."

Awesome.

I nodded my head and climbed the old stairs that led into the house. I could do this. I kept telling myself that over and over. I was strong enough to face him. I was more than capable of pretending like I was completely and utterly unaffected by him.

Even though I had barely left my bed over the past week.

I could hear him working as soon as I stepped through the door, and I closed my eyes and took a deep breath as I pushed the door closed behind me. Josie and Frankie had offered to take over my community service duties for the rest of my time with Carson, but it didn't work that way.

Not only would Mr. Sneed not allow it, but there was no way I would let them do all this work for something I did.

Because at the end of the day, I was the one who agreed to sneak into this property with Carson, and I was the one who had let him touch me so inappropriately in this house. I was the one who had trusted him even though he had proven to me time and again that he wasn't worthy of it.

He was squatted down and running a paint scraper over the wall as I walked in. He was dripping with sweat, and he was wearing nothing but a pair of old jeans and tennis shoes. His discarded shirt was laying on the dirty floor with his bottle of water, and I wished he would put it back on.

Jerk or not, he was still one of the most attractive guys I had ever seen.

"Where do I need to start?"

He jumped, the sound of my voice clearly scaring him, and I found myself grinning when he almost landed on his ass.

"Allie," he said my name like it meant something to him, like I meant something to him, but I knew that was just another one of his games. Carson was the master of fucking with my head, and that was what he did every single time he called me and text me and showed up at my house since the moment I left our camping trip.

He fucked with my head.

But I no longer trusted anything about him or anything he said or did.

"It looks like you've already finished the living room." I looked over my shoulder to avoid looking at him and his sad eyes. "I can start in the hallway."

He stepped toward me and reached out his hand before thinking better of it and dropping it to his side. "Can we talk?"

"About what?" I sounded so disinterested, and I knew that he heard it too.

"About us."

I laughed and tucked my hands in my back pockets. "There is no us, Carson. Do you have an extra paint scraper, or do I need to go get one from Mr. Sneed?"

He clenched his jaw and watched me, and I knew that he wanted to argue. It wasn't an argument that he would win. "I have an extra."

He bent down to scoop up the tool, then handed it out to me. I grabbed it, careful not to touch him, but he refused to let go.

"Drop it, Carson," I growled at him.

"I don't want to." I knew he wasn't talking about the tool, but I didn't care what he wanted. I used to care, I cared more than anything, but not anymore.

"It doesn't matter what you want." I shrugged and jerked the tool from his hand. "Or is this about more than me and you?" I looked around the room dramatically. "If you need me to do something for you to win a bet, please let me know so we don't have to draw this out."

"You know this isn't about any stupid bet."

"I don't know anything." I could feel my heartbeat rising,

and I was so damn angry with him. "And I cannot trust a word you say. Should I call Eli?"

"Don't." He shook his head, and there was so much anger hidden in his eyes. But he had no right to be angry. He didn't have the right to feel anything.

"Don't what?" I laughed and walked away from him. "I can do whatever I want, Carson. It's not up to you."

"Not with him."

I spun around to find him following me, and I waved my hand in his direction, pointing the paint scraper right at him. "You don't get a say in whether or not I do anything with him. If I wanted to, I would leave here right now and go fuck him."

"I will kill him."

"For what?" I held my hands out as I tried to grasp exactly what the heck was going through his head. "Doing the exact same thing you did? You took my virginity. You won the bet. What else could you possibly want?"

"I know that I fucked up." He ran his hand over his sweaty hair. "But I am not him. I did what I did to keep him away from you. I tried to tell you what they had planned but you didn't listen. I knew the only way to get you to stay away from him was to get you to spend time with me. I didn't think..."

"You didn't think." I held on to the tool so tightly that my knuckles turned white. I wasn't ready to face him. I wasn't ready to have this conversation about what I thought we were and what we actually became. "You aren't some hero, Carson. You hurt me because you wanted to. You hurt me because you have some fucked-up grudge against me because of your own parents."

"Don't go there, Allie."

"I can go wherever I want." I raised my voice but tried to remind myself to calm down. He didn't deserve to see how affected I was by him. He and Eli and everyone else at the campground had already gotten to see how affected I was when I found out the truth. "I have tiptoed over talking about our past with you for so long that I'm freaking sick of it. I wasn't the one who cheated on your mom, and I wasn't the one who tried to kill herself, Carson."

He winced, and I knew I should have stopped. But this was a conversation we should have had a long time ago.

"I was your friend and you pushed me away because you needed someone to put the blame on for how hurt you were. I used to be fine with taking that from you, but I'm not anymore." I straightened my spine. "Grow the hell up, Carson."

I turned my back on him again when he didn't reply and headed to the hallway, even though being in this house with him was the absolute last place I wanted to be.

But I stopped dead in my tracks at the next sound of his voice.

"If he touches you, I'll kill him."

"What?" I looked over my shoulder, and he was staring at me like he actually meant what he was saying.

"Eli. If he lays a single finger on you, I will kill him."

Then he walked back the way he came, and I focused on my work.

CHAPTER 2
CARSON

I was so damn ready for this day to be over.

I couldn't focus on what our teacher was talking about. I hadn't heard a single word from her in over an hour. Instead, I tapped my pencil against my notebook and tried not to think about Allie.

But that was impossible.

Every single thought I had these days was about her. About how badly I had fucked things up with her. I obsessed over how mad she was, over how I could possibly get her to forgive me, and how I couldn't sleep because she wouldn't talk to me.

The final bell rang, and I snatched my shit up from my desk and was out of the room before anyone else. I felt like I was suffocating in there.

I was suffocating everywhere except when I was with her, and even then, it was torturous. Because she refused to even speak to me.

Not since that first day she came back to our community

service, and I was pretty sure I was running out of those silent days with her. Mr. Sneed hadn't yet told us when he was going to let us off the hook for our community service, but the house was already looking like a different place altogether.

He told us yesterday that he would have paint ready for us to paint over the signature wall when we got there tomorrow, and I was dreading it. She had done nothing but nodded her head, then left without a single word to me.

Mr. Sneed had given me a look of sympathy, and I knew that I was really fucked then.

I pushed through the locker room, and it was still silent. I shoved my shit into my locker before pulling out my practice gear. Being at baseball practice was the last place I wanted to be, but I knew that it would do me good.

It would take away some of that pent-up anger I couldn't seem to get under control. Even smoking and drinking hadn't helped, and trust me, I had tried. Olly was still a little pissed off after he had to take care of my drunk ass last weekend.

But as soon as I woke up the next morning, I had felt exactly the same. Worse almost.

And part of me had thought about just taking any girl up on their offer and trying my hardest to fuck the thoughts of Allie away, but I couldn't. Just thinking about it made me sick.

I couldn't do it after everything that had happened between us. Even if she hated me now. I didn't know how I could possibly touch another girl again, and that fucked with my head more than anything.

I was so damn wrapped up in her that nothing that used to matter to me mattered anymore.

I had been so worried about not getting too dependent on her and her on me that I didn't realize I was falling for her all along while simultaneously pushing her away. Now I was the one who needed her, and she didn't need or want a single thing from me.

The guys started filtering into the locker room, and I took a deep breath as I tried to prepare myself to face them. Eli and Lucas smirked and dug at me any chance they could. They knew that I had fucked up and that their stupid little fucking plan had been my downfall all along.

Beck and Olly had wanted to kill Eli after he told Allie the truth about what I had done, but it was pointless. He was telling her the damn truth while I was hiding it from her. I had painted him as the villain, but he wasn't any more villainous than I was.

Allie had been my best friend once, and I had still chosen to go through with my fucked-up plan. It didn't matter that I had started it as a way to keep them away from her; I knew what I was doing. I was desperate to be around her, to have an excuse to have her in my life again, and I took advantage of the situation.

And when things changed, when they had become more, I should have been honest with her, but I wasn't. And I took things too far.

I took things from her that I didn't deserve. She gave those things to me, and I knew she regretted that decision now.

And that was what hurt the most out of all of this. Allie had given me her body, her trust, she had given me things that she hadn't ever given to anyone else, and I ruined every bit of it.

And even though I wanted to kill both Eli and Lucas, I

knew that it was my fault. I could blame them all I wanted but everything that happened between Allie and me was my fault. I knew that fact as well as she did.

Because Allie hadn't even looked at Eli after she found out. His betrayal hadn't bothered her at all. It was me and my lies that had broken her. It was me and my lies that had fucked everything up.

I would always fuck everything up when it came to her. That was who I was. Eli may not have been good enough for her, but neither was I.

"What are you doing?" Beck tossed his bag down on the bench before opening his own locker and pulling out his gear.

"Just getting ready for practice." I pulled on my cleats and tried to focus on tying the laces. I tried to focus on anything other than the repetitive what-ifs that ran through my head. "Where's Olly?"

"I don't know." Beck threw his button-down into the locker before pulling an old t-shirt over his head. "He's been a bit distant lately. I think something might be going on with him."

I winced because, who the hell didn't have something going on at this point? But also, because I knew that the only thing Olly wanted to have going on was something with Frankie, and that was never going to happen. "Hopefully he's just getting laid or something."

"I was hoping that you'd be the one getting laid." Beck pulled his cleats out of his locker and sat down beside me. "You've been in a bad fucking mood."

"Yeah. I'm aware." I looked over at my best friend and part of me just wanted to unload everything on him, but this wasn't the time or the place. And I wasn't sure if I was willing to let Beck or Olly in on all the shit I had going on in my head. "But I don't really think getting laid is the answer right now."

"Since when?" Beck looked at me, really looked at me, and I knew that he was trying to figure out what was going through my head. Beck always knew when something was off with me. "You know if you fuck things up further with Allie that the girls are going to kill you, right?"

"To be honest, I really don't care what the girls think." I shrugged my shoulders because it was the truth. I loved Frankie and Josie, but their opinions didn't really matter when it came to Allie. I knew that they only wanted what was best for her, but I also knew that neither one of them believed that was me. "But I don't think there's a chance for me to fuck things up further. Allie is refusing to even speak to me."

"Well, you're going to have to figure out how to get past that, or you're going to have to give up." Beck stood and closed his locker. "Those are your two options."

"You say that like it's easy."

"Hell no. It isn't easy." He paused and nodded to one of our teammates as they walked by. He waited until he was around the corner before he spoke again. "But that's your reality. It was the same reality I had to face with Josie. She's either worth the work to get her to forgive you or she isn't, and you're the only one who can decide that."

"But Josie was head over heels in love with you before you fucked everything up."

He nodded his head and crossed his arms. "And Allie was with you. You don't think we all realized that Allie's been into you long before the two of you pushed each other away, then started making your way back to each other? Whatever you did, and I mean beyond that stupid fucking bet, you need to fix it. You need to fix it and make sure she knows that the two of you are worth it."

"And if she doesn't?"

"Make her."

"I don't think Allie can be made to do anything," I grumbled and grabbed my glove. Beck followed me out of the locker room and onto the field.

There were already a couple of our teammates throwing by the time we got out there, but Olly was nowhere to be seen. I pulled my cell phone out of my pocket and sent him a quick text asking him where he was.

Beck and I started throwing, and several minutes later, Olly finally pushed through the locker room door and out onto the field.

He was pissed. I knew that the moment I saw him, and Olly rarely got pissed enough to show his emotions.

"What's wrong?" I asked him as soon as he tossed his baseball bag down on the ground and shoved his left hand in his glove.

"Nothing. Throw me the ball." He hit the inside of his glove, indicating for me to throw it, and I threw the ball to him even though I knew he was lying.

He pulled the ball out of his glove and threw it back to me a lot harder than necessary. I didn't say anything, though. I simply caught the ball, then threw it to Beck. I could see Beck watching Olly too. He knew he was lying just as well as I did.

"Why are your knuckles bloody?" As soon as the question passed Beck's lips, Lucas and Eli walked out onto the field.

I saw Olly wince before I saw anything else. But then I

saw Eli's face. He was pissed too. Angrier than Olly, and he was also sporting a split lip that still had fresh blood pooling around it.

I looked from him to Olly, and I couldn't help noticing how Olly clenched his fist at his side.

"I'm warm," I called to the two of them, even though we had barely thrown, before jogging up beside Olly.

"What the fuck happened?" My question was quiet because the last thing we needed was for Coach to hear us. He would hand us our asses before our practice even began.

"I said, nothing." Olly tried to shrug us off, but neither Beck nor I were having any of that.

"Something happened." I nodded toward Eli who had moved as far from us as he could possibly get to warm up. He looked up in our direction as he ran the back of his hand against his lip. "Did you do that to him?"

"I did." Olly grabbed his bag, and Beck and I followed him to the dugout.

"And?" Beck asked the question we were both thinking.

"And he deserved it. He was talking shit, and I just couldn't stand it anymore." Olly tossed his bag down on the bench.

"Talking shit about what?" I was pretty certain I already knew. If I had to bet, I would say that Eli was talking shit about me or Allie or a combination of the two of us. It was the only thing that guy had to brag about these days.

"Allie," Olly confirmed, and my pulse spiked. "Allie gave him nothing and hasn't spoken to him since that day at the campground, but he's walking around talking like he bagged her. He was telling a few of the guys some bullshit story in the hallway, and I couldn't stand it."

"He was telling people that Allie slept with him?" I could

hear my own anger. I could feel it pulsing through every part of me. This anger was so much easier than the anger I felt toward myself. I could mold it, control it, do something about it.

And I was going to.

"Carson." Beck put his hand on my chest, but I didn't need him to calm me down. I needed Olly to tell me exactly what he said.

"Yeah." Olly nodded, and I knew from the look in his eyes he was thinking about lying to me with what he said next. He realized how easily triggered I was. "But he won't talk about her again. He hit that locker so hard when my fist connected with his jaw that I think he was dazed for a second. He didn't even try to hit me back."

"What the fuck did he say, Olly?" I stared at him because I wasn't fucking around. I wanted to know exactly what that piece of shit was saying about my girl.

"He was just telling them about how you had his sloppy seconds. That he paved the way for you to get inside her."

I didn't wait around to hear another word. I stormed out of the dugout and headed straight for Eli. I didn't care that the rest of the team was still warming up or that Coach was standing there with his clipboard going over our roster. I pushed through all of them until I was face to face with Eli, and he looked up at me with that fucking smirk on his face.

That fucking smirk that was going to get him killed.

"What is it, Hale?" He tossed the ball in the air before catching it back into his mitt. "Are you butt-hurt like your little buddy in there? It's not my fault that Allie dropped your ass after you couldn't give her what she needed."

"Don't say her fucking name again." I stepped toward

him, and there was the slightest flash of fear in his eyes. "Don't talk about her at all."

"What's going on here?" I could hear Coach coming up behind me, but I couldn't care less about him at that moment.

He could punish me however he wanted. He could kick my ass off the team if that's what it took, but I wasn't walking away from Eli until I made it perfectly clear where I stood when it came to Allie.

"Oh shit, my man." Eli laughed and put his hand over his chest. "I thought this was all about a bet. I didn't realize the girl had you fucking whipped."

Laughter rang out around us just as Coach came into view.

"The two of you back away from each other. I don't know what the hell is going on here, but my field isn't the time or place for it."

"Don't tell people that you slept with her when you and I both know that she didn't let you touch her." I didn't know why the thought of him telling everyone bothered me so much. Of course, I didn't want anyone to think badly of Allie, but I also couldn't stand the thought of anyone thinking that she had ever been anyone's other than mine.

"Is that what she told you?" He cocked his head just slightly as if he was analyzing me. "She really is a filthy little whore, isn't she?"

The last words were barely out of his mouth when I barreled into him and tackled him to the ground. My shoulder slammed into his midsection as his back hit the ground, but I didn't have time to think about the ache that already started there. Eli had already thrown his glove to the ground and was throwing punches.

His fist connected with my jaw, then my elbow connected with his nose. After that, it was nothing but a chaos of fists and elbows and jabs and grunts. Eli managed to get himself flipped over me, and he rained down punch after punch into my face and chest.

I barely felt a single one of them.

I caught his fist in my hand and threw a right hook into the side of his head that seemed to stun him. I could hear yelling around us, but I didn't let them stop me. I threw Eli off me, and I continued to throw punches until I felt the crunch of bone beneath my knuckles.

Even then, I didn't stop.

I didn't stop until someone's arms wrapped around my torso and jerked me off of him.

"Fucking stop." Coach's booming voice finally registered then, and I went slack against Beck. "Get him the fuck out of here."

He pointed toward me, and one of the assistant coaches moved in my direction. I shrugged Beck off of me and held up my hands when they looked like they thought I might attack again.

Eli was sitting up and he shoved one of the guys off him that was trying to help him up.

"Remember what I said, Eli." I walked backward away from him in the direction that the assistant coach was leading me. "You talk about her again, and I'll finish wrecking that face of yours."

"Carson, shut your mouth." Coach pointed at me, and his face was so red that he looked like he would have a heart attack at any moment. "You're about to find your ass riding the bench for the rest of the year."

"I don't give a fuck." I looked him in the eye because I

didn't. I knew that baseball was important and that I had scholarships to play in college, but none of it mattered at that moment. I couldn't see past anything but Allie and Eli and the thought of him touching her.

I would give up everything to make sure that he never spoke of her or touched her again.

CHAPTER 3
ALLIE

I walked through the hallway of my school, and I could feel people looking at me. At first, I thought it was in my head, but then I overheard some girls talking about me in the bathroom.

The news of the bet had made it all the way to Clermont High, and I obviously wasn't the only victim of the bet. There were a few other girls from High and several from Prep, but apparently, the bet that involved me specifically was a little more interesting than the others.

And I had heard it all so far. Both Eli and Carson had managed to sleep with me before the bet's time limit, neither of them had, and I even heard one guy whispering that he had heard it ended in a threesome.

I couldn't do anything but roll my eyes.

I had no idea where these people got their information, but none of it could be further from the truth. I hadn't even spoken to Eli since I left that campground even though he had text me to apologize on multiple occasions.

I didn't reply to a single one of them.

Because his apologies didn't matter one way or another to me. Not when I was so focused on Carson.

And I knew that wasn't fair. They were equally guilty in entering the bet. If what Carson said was true, Eli was even more so, but I didn't trust Eli. I didn't care about him.

"Hey, Allie." I looked up from my phone to see Will Hollis leaning next to my locker. He had his thumbs hooked in the straps of his backpack, and he looked nervous. Will was nice. He always had been, but I hated how my stomach dropped seeing him there.

"Hey, Will. What's up?" I opened my locker and shoved my books in before grabbing the ones I needed for my homework tonight.

"I just wanted to check on you." He lowered his voice and leaned in closer to me. "The shit I've been hearing around school has been pretty rough."

"Most of it isn't true." I shrugged and tried to play the whole situation off. "But thank you for checking on me."

"You're welcome." He turned toward me and crossed his arms. "You should come out this weekend. We're planning on having a party down on the north beach."

I nodded my head because I used to go to the beach parties all the time, but it had been a while since I had been to one. "I'll think about it. I just have a lot going on."

"No. I get it." He smiled. "Is work busy as hell right now?"

"Work's busy, trying to keep my grades up, then finishing out my community service."

"I heard about that." He laughed. "I was a little shocked to find out that you are the one who got in trouble, but hey, we all have our wild streaks."

"Not a wild streak." I smiled and closed my locker. "It was just a major lapse in judgment."

"We've all been there." He held up his hand for a high five, and I couldn't help smiling as I slapped my hand against his.

Will was so damn wholesome and nice, and he didn't have to be. He was also hot, incredibly so, and I had no idea how he was still single. He should have been scooped up long before now.

"You know where the party is but text me if you need anything." He shot a finger gun at me, and I laughed as I hiked my bag onto my shoulder and turned in the other direction.

"Maybe she's sleeping with all three of them," I heard a girl whisper from across the hall, and I told myself to ignore it. It didn't matter what they thought of me. I knew the truth.

And that truth was so much sadder than any of them realized.

"I wouldn't put it past her," another snickered, and my spine straightened. I used to be friends with these girls, or at least friendly enough. But people were quick to drop you when they thought they knew you better than you knew yourself. They had heard a few stupid rumors and suddenly they were all experts.

But they forgot that I already knew some of their secrets. Secrets that they had told me themselves. Secrets I would never share because I wasn't like them. I would never be like them.

I pushed outside of the school and took a deep breath as I walked to my car. I was due to be at community service in an hour and a half, but I needed to do something, anything to take the edge off the rising panic that was filling inside of me.

Knowing that I was going to see Carson soon did that to

me because I didn't know what to expect. I had been avoiding him as much as I could while we were there. I absolutely refused to speak to him, but he didn't care.

He was far from ignoring me.

I felt like he watched every single move I made.

I hadn't seen him in a couple days. He had baseball practice yesterday which got us both out of community service, and even though I was dreading seeing him now, I would be lying if I said that I enjoyed being away from him.

It was like my own personal hell.

I wanted to be around him almost as much as I wanted to avoid him. But I guess it had been like that with Carson for a really long time.

I rolled down my windows and let the air rush through my hair. It felt good. It was finally starting to cool down, and I soaked in the feel of the breeze mixed with the warm glow of the sun as I drove away from my school.

I drove and I drove, and by the time I actually looked down at the clock again, I was almost late.

Carson was already there by the time I arrived, but that had become the norm. He was always here working away when I arrived. He acted like he actually took this seriously, like he actually cared what Mr. Sneed thought.

Even though Mr. Sneed didn't give us any indication over whether or not he was happy with the work we were doing or if he planned on letting us stop any time soon. I think the old man had half a mind to keep us working as long as he could get away with it.

Carson didn't say anything as I walked into the house. He was on his knees near the door, and he was sanding the old antique baseboards that were covered in years' worth of paint. I set my bag down on the stairs and watched him as he worked.

He didn't utter a word or so much as look in my direction, and I should have been happy. This was what I had been wanting for days, but it didn't feel like what I wanted.

His shirt was clinging to his back with sweat, and he was sanding the board down like it had personally pissed him off. I grabbed the other block of sandpaper and dropped to my knees beside him. He kept working like he didn't notice my presence at all.

I ran my sandpaper over the wood and tried to ignore him like he was ignoring me, but I couldn't. I looked up at him, and it was then that I noticed his black eye and swollen bottom lip.

I dropped the sandpaper and reached out for him before I thought better of it and caught myself. My hand was so close to his face, and he finally looked up at me then.

His eye was worse than I thought. The bruising went down onto his cheekbone, and there was so much swelling that I was surprised his eye wasn't swollen shut.

"What happened to you?" I pulled my hand away before I did something stupid and touched him, and he watched it retreat.

"Had an altercation." His answer was curt.

"I can see that." I cocked my head to the side to get a good look at him. The skin of his knuckles was broken and some of them were bruised, and I hated that he had been in a fight. "With anyone in particular?"

"Do you really want to know?" He spit out the question as he continued to sand, and I was shocked by his anger.

"I wouldn't have asked if I didn't want to know. Who did that to you?" I pointed to his eye.

"Well, technically you could say I did it to myself since I was the one who threw the first punch, but this black eye I'm sporting is courtesy of your little boyfriend."

"You got in a fight with Eli?" I don't know why that shocked me so much, but it did.

"Of course, you knew exactly who I was talking about," he grumbled.

"Don't be a baby." I looked down at his knuckles. "You know good and well that he's not my boyfriend."

"Does everyone else know that?" He finally looked up at me again.

"What the heck is that supposed to mean?" I didn't care what anyone else knew, and he usually didn't either.

He dropped his sandpaper to the ground and stood. He was covered in dust, and it fell around him as he started pacing the room. "It means that he's telling everyone at school that the two of you slept together."

"Okay?" I had heard the rumor too, but I didn't know that it had come straight from the ass's mouth.

"Okay?" Carson laughed without a trace of humor. "So did you sleep with him?"

"Are you seriously asking me that?" I stood and faced him.

"Yes. I am." He crossed his arms, and if I didn't know him so well, I would have been intimidated. But this version of Carson was the broken boy that I had known for longer than any other version of him. He was insecure and latching on to whatever truth made the most sense to him. Whatever truth he expected other people to let him down with.

"No. I didn't sleep with him, you asshole." I turned on my heel and headed toward the door, but he stopped me with his hand on mine.

"I didn't mean—"

"What, Carson?" I looked back at him over my shoulder. "You didn't mean to assume that I slept with another guy right after I gave you my virginity or that I had lied to you and slept with him before?"

"I didn't think you slept with him at all." His fingers tightened around mine almost to the point of pain. "I just got so fucking angry listening to the shit he said, and it started fucking with my head."

"What Eli says doesn't matter. I don't care what he says about me."

"But I do." He looked so lost in that moment, so at odds with the normal, cocky Carson I had become used to. "I can't stand the thought of other people thinking that he had touched you, that he had been inside you."

I jerked my hand out of his and stepped away as I turned to face him. "I'm not some fucking trophy, Carson. It's not going to tarnish your precious reputation if people think someone else fucked something that you believe once belonged to you."

"I don't give a shit about my reputation."

"Don't you?" I was becoming so angry that part of me was happy he got that black eye. "Why else would you start a fight with Eli? You two had a bet and you won. Congratulations, Carson."

He took a step toward me before stopping himself. "I got in a fight with him because I hate that he even had a chance at touching you. I hate that he kissed you. I hate that I agreed to that stupid fucking bet to begin with." He stepped closer to me again. "I hate that I ever gave him the chance to hurt you."

"He didn't hurt me." I looked him over, and I wished that

he knew what he had always meant to me. I wished that we could go back and change the way our future had become. "You are the one who accomplished that."

"And I told you that I'm sorry."

"My sorrys have never been good enough for you, so what makes you think yours will ever be good enough for me?" I hated that truth, but I couldn't hide it either.

He had hated me for so long and for much less than what he did to me.

He stormed toward me, and I didn't have time to think let alone move before he pressed against me and backed me into the wall. I tried to catch my breath as his battered hand cupped my cheek.

"You know that's not true." He shook his head. "I've been so fucked up, Allie, and I shouldn't have ever put any of that on you."

I could barely swallow as he spoke, and he ran his hand over my neck and followed the movement. I could feel my pulse beating rapidly beneath his fingers. "It doesn't matter."

"Yes. It does." He leaned in closer to me, and I didn't move away.

It was stupid and reckless, but I couldn't move away from him. Not when he was like this. He pressed his lips to mine, gently at first, then more harshly. It was as if that first touch set off a frenzy inside of him.

He kissed me like he had missed every inch of me. His hand tightened on my neck and the other tangled into my hair. I kissed him back just as hard.

I put every bit of anger and hurt into the kiss, and I hoped he felt it. I hoped that he knew this wasn't some kiss that was going to make things better for us. I wasn't sure that even existed.

There wasn't anything that could take back the things that had been done.

His teeth pressed into my bottom lip before he sucked it into his mouth, and I couldn't stop the small whimper that passed my lips.

There was an ache deep in my belly, an ache that only he had ever fixed, and I hated that one simple kiss could make me want him so badly. My legs trembled beneath me, and my heart felt like it didn't even belong to me.

As much as I hated him, I was still so turned on by him. I wanted him regardless of everything that happened.

He pressed his hips into mine, and I felt how badly he wanted me too. It would be so easy to forget everything and give into each other. I didn't need some grand gesture of love for me to fall apart under Carson's hands, but I also knew that I couldn't keep things separate either. The moment he touched me, him touching me now, it messed with my heart.

My chest ached as badly as the low ache in my stomach. My body was completely at war with itself.

If I gave into Carson now, I would hate him even more later. I would hate myself. Because no matter what happened or what he felt, I was in love with Carson Hale, and I was only at risk of falling deeper and deeper for him.

I was going to continue to fall, and he wouldn't. I would fall and it would shred me apart.

Because Carson wasn't the kind of guy I was meant to fall for. He wasn't some knight in shining armor who was going to give me my happily ever after. I used to think he was, but I was so damn foolish.

The boy I used to daydream about and the boy touching me now were two different people. They were night and day, and I needed to draw the line of who he is and who he was in my head.

Right now, everything was muddy and nothing about us was clear, and every time I allowed something like this to happen, it only became worse.

I pushed against his chest, and Carson reluctantly pulled away from me. His breathing was harsh and mingled with mine, and he looked as lost as I was.

"We can't do this." My voice was barely a whisper between us, but it felt so heavy on my tongue.

"Allie." He caressed my cheek, but I pulled away.

"No." I pushed harder against him and didn't look back as I walked away from him and out of the old house.

CHAPTER 4
CARSON

We walked into the country club, and I knew she was there. Her car was parked outside, along with Josie's, and Olly had tried to talk us into going somewhere else.

When we took a seat in the restaurant, it was all I could do to search every inch of the space looking for her, but I didn't see her anywhere.

"I can't believe Coach benched you. How long did he say again?" Beck asked.

"Two weeks." I heard the kitchen door open and looked toward it, but it wasn't her.

"That seems a bit harsh, but I guess it could be a lot worse."

"Yeah." Olly nodded. "You're lucky he kept it between the team. The school would have probably suspended you both."

"What about you?" Beck nodded toward Olly.

"No one saw us." Olly chuckled. "I didn't make a grand event out of it like Carson."

They both chuckled and I rolled my eyes. "It's not like I was planning it. Actually, I should really blame it on you. If you hadn't come to practice so pissed, I wouldn't have even gotten in trouble, asshole."

"Okay," Olly said sarcastically and leaned back in his chair. "I had just defended your girl's honor, but please, blame it on me."

I was obviously joking, but when I looked over at him, I realized that I never did thank him for that. "You're right." I held out my fist, and he bumped his against it. "Thank you for that."

"No problem. I doubt Eli will be talking shit again anytime soon."

"I don't know." Beck was checking his phone but put it down on the table. "He seems like a pretty big idiot, and he's friends with Lucas. God knows he's not going to be making any smart decisions."

"This is true," I said just as Josie walked up to the table.

"Hey, guys." She grinned down at Beck. "What can I get you all to drink?"

Beck grabbed the edge of her apron and pulled her toward him. He didn't give her any time to object as he pulled her down and pressed his lips to hers.

"Beck," she huffed and straightened. "I'm at work."

"So?" He looked up at her like she was crazy.

"So, I'd like to not get fired."

We all chuckled because we knew that was never going to happen. Even if Beck's dad didn't own the place, Josie was a good worker and Mr. Clermont adored her.

"Now what do you all want to drink?"

"Water."

"Same," Olly answered.

"Is Allie here?" I leaned back in my chair and wished I never opened my big mouth.

Josie narrowed her eyes at me. "She is."

I nodded and tried to appear disinterested, but I wasn't fooling anyone. "Like, in the restaurant?"

Josie grinned this time before she spoke. "The last time I saw her she was back there in the kitchen making out with the hot new cook we got."

Beck swatted at her leg, and she grimaced. "Ow."

I knew she was fucking with me, but my heart still raced at her words.

"Don't fuck around, Josie. He just got benched for fighting for her honor. I'd hate to see what he'd do if he actually caught another guy touching her." Olly looked over at me. "He's volatile now that she broke his heart."

"She didn't break my heart," I grumbled, and they all three of them looked at me like they didn't believe a single word I said.

"Didn't she?" Josie put her hands on her hips. "From the outside looking in, it looks like the two of you broke each other's hearts."

"Well, since you're so knowledgeable, do you think I have even the slightest chance of fixing things?"

"I don't know." She watched me. "And I honestly don't know if I want you to. You've been a complete and total jerk to her."

"I know." We all did.

"And then you somehow convinced her to like you again after you've treated her like shit for as long as I've known you."

"Yeah."

"Then you broke her again."

"I didn't mean to. I…"

"It doesn't matter what you meant to do. It's what happened, and clinging to the fact that it's not what you intended to happen is going to get you nowhere. If you want to get her back, you need to prove that you aren't this asshole that you've made her believe you are."

"I thought you didn't want me to get her back."

"I said I didn't know." She pointed at me. "I'm not sure if I trust you with her again."

"But you're going to give me a chance?"

"It's not my chance to give. I will stand by whatever decision Allie makes. If she says you're a piece of shit, then you're a piece of shit."

"Okay." I chuckled. "That's fair."

"But, if you hurt her again, I swear on my life that Beck is going to kick your ass."

I looked over at my best friend as he winced.

"Deal. If I hurt her again, I will gladly get my ass kicked by him."

"Good." She took a step back. "Now let me go get your drinks."

As soon as she walked away, I spotted Allie behind the bar. She was laughing with the bartender as she placed some drinks onto her tray. She looked so damn beautiful.

Her hair was tied back away from her face, and she was in her plain uniform that the rest of the staff wore. But it didn't look plain on her. It looked anything but.

She lifted the tray in her hand and laughed as she walked away from the bar. She hadn't looked up at me, and I didn't know if she was aware I was here. I figured Josie would have told her, warned her, but she was walking through the restaurant like she didn't have a care in the world.

And it could simply be that she didn't care that I was here at all, but I had to believe that wasn't it.

After I kissed her at community service yesterday, she looked so torn, so hurt, and I wanted to do anything I possibly could to take that look away from her. But she didn't give me a chance. She ran before I could say or do anything.

I had told Mr. Sneed that she had gotten sick. I knew that he didn't believe me. He made that perfectly clear, but I had stayed an extra hour to make up for her being gone.

She went to a table a few away from us, and she smiled at the guests as she sat their alcohol down in front of them. I watched her as she worked. She was so good at her job, so friendly and personable, and it made me wonder what she was going to go on to do.

Allie was capable of doing or being whatever it was she wanted, but I didn't think she believed that. I had probably helped plant any seeds of doubt that she had.

And I wished that I could take every second of that away.

I wished that I could take back so much of what I had done and said, but I couldn't. The only thing I could do now was be different for her, but I didn't know if I was capable of that.

She walked away from the table and her steps faltered when her gaze finally landed on me. She looked around the table quickly before storming toward where I sat.

"What are you doing here?" she hissed, and I knew that she was still pissed about yesterday or everything that happened before yesterday. Either way, she wasn't happy to see me.

"Eating dinner." I motioned around us as if that fact should have been obvious. That only pissed her off more.

"There are a hundred different restaurants in this town. Couldn't you all have found somewhere else to go?"

"In all fairness, my dad owns this place, so we come here a lot."

Allie's gaze snapped to Beck, and he quickly shut up.

"I didn't realize that you worked tonight," I lied to her. "I also didn't realize that it was such a big issue for you to see me."

"Well, now you know." She tucked the tray she was carrying under her arm. "I'm already forced to do community service with you. You could at least give me a night off."

"Forced?" I raised an eyebrow at her, and I knew I should have stopped talking, but getting a rise out of her was so entertaining and such a damn turn on. "I thought you were enjoying our time together."

"Wrong." Her answer was instant.

Josie walked up behind her and looked back and forth between us before sitting our drinks on the table.

"You didn't enjoy what happened yesterday?"

"What happened yesterday?" Josie asked, and I watched as Allie's face reddened.

"Nothing happened."

"It most certainly did." I looked back and forth between them. "Allie might be pissed at me, but she didn't stop me from kissing her."

"That's a lie. I did stop you."

"After you thoroughly enjoyed it." God, it had felt like she enjoyed it.

"Then I came to my senses and realized that I was kissing the asshole who had just broke me." Her fist was clenched at her side, and she was staring directly at me. "Don't worry. I will never let it happen again."

"It will." I said it with so much power because I truly meant it. I would do whatever it took to make sure it did.

"No. It won't." She finally looked away from me and around the table. "Go ahead and make bets about it if you need to. It's not going to happen."

Then she stormed away from the table and back to the kitchen.

Josie sighed, and I looked away from Allie's retreating form to look up at her. "I had, like, the tiniest bit of faith that you could pull this off, but you lost that. If you all take bets, put me down for a hundred on him not getting the girl."

Then she flipped me off.

CHAPTER 5
ALLIE

I was pissed.

More than pissed, actually. I was so angry that I couldn't think straight and spending another day alone with Carson was the absolute last thing I wanted to do.

Because I knew that getting under my skin had become a dang game to him.

He pushes and pushes until I can't take anymore, then he laps up my anger like it's a damn drug to him.

I managed to get to community service before he arrived, and I was glad. I didn't have the energy to deal with him or avoid talking to him as I tried to start whatever job Mr. Sneed wanted us to do today.

I walked up to the front door, and there was a note taped to it. I rolled my eyes at Mr. Sneed's writing, where he thanked Carson for something he had done to the original woodwork before asking us to start working on the kitchen.

I left the note where it was so Carson could see it, then I walked into the house. It was pretty creepy without Carson here, but there was no way in hell I was going to stand there and wait on him and give him any sort of ammunition over me. No. I was just going to pull up my big girl panties, check behind me every five seconds, and get to work.

I was doing exactly that by the time Carson walked in. He was singing the lyrics to some song I didn't know, and I tried to ignore him as I used the broom to sweep all the cobwebs that covered almost every inch of the forgotten kitchen.

"Hello." Carson's friendly tone made my back straighten and my heart race.

I nodded in his direction but didn't respond. My heart was racing, but I tried not to let it show.

"Okay." He chuckled and turned away from me. He started working. I had no idea what he was doing, but I also didn't care. I wasn't here to worry about Carson or the way he may or may not have made me feel. Or what it was like when I kissed him the other day.

Nope. I definitely wasn't here to think about kissing him again.

It wasn't running through my mind over and over and tying my stomach into knots.

"Did someone piss you off?" Finally, he looked back up at me.

I wasn't thinking as I moved toward him and shoved against his chest. My fingers trembled along with my nerves. Dealing with Carson Hale was no longer something I wanted to do. I was so tired of his game of hot and cold. I was so exhausted trying to figure out what he wanted and didn't want from me.

"Allie," he said my name and made it sound like more

than it was. I pushed him again, forcing his back to hit the wall in the hallway because that only pissed me off more. I felt that one simple word like it was racing through me, chasing something I didn't have. "Fuck. Stop hitting me."

"I'm not hitting you," I hissed the words between my teeth because I wanted to hit him. I wanted to take every bit of aggression I felt out on him because it was all his fault.

He snatched my hand in his before I could push him again and held it against his chest. "What do you call that then?"

I tried to tug my hand back from him, but he refused to let go. He held my hand firmly against his chest as he scowled down at me. Every bit of the playfulness from earlier was gone.

"I call it pushing you away." I tilted my head to the side and stared at him. "You should recognize that from a mile away. You're the king of it, aren't you?"

Finally, there was a trace of a smile on his lips, and it was all I needed to flame my anger. He was so damn cocky and sure that he was exactly what everyone else wanted, but he was wrong.

I wanted nothing to do with him. Not anymore. Not after everything happened and still continued to mess with my head. He made me weak, and I refused to be that girl anymore.

I refused to allow him to use me and my heart as nothing more than a toy for him to play with.

Because that was exactly what I had been all along.

"You're the one who has been pushing me away lately, remember?"

"No." I shook my head and tugged on my hand again. "I

remember you being a complete and total asshole and ruining anything that might have happened between us."

"You mean, what did happen between us."

"No. I meant everything that you faked. Nothing that happened was real. None of it mattered." My chest ached as I spoke the words, but I knew they were true. As badly as I wished they weren't, that was my reality.

I had handed things over to Carson that he didn't deserve. He played me and I fell into it effortlessly. It didn't matter what he said about Eli. Carson was the devil in disguise. He was the one who burned me so damn easily without even trying.

Eli never stood a chance.

Not against him.

"Don't say that." He jerked my hand closer and forced my feet to stumble forward toward him. My other hand pressed against his chest to try to maintain distance between us. I couldn't risk being so close to him that I couldn't keep my head clear.

Being close to him did more than just mess with my head. It messed with every single part of me. My heart raced and I felt like I was falling. He was like my center of gravity and no matter how badly I wished he wasn't, I was drawn to him.

It didn't matter what he did or said or how badly he treated me, I was drawn to him in a way that I couldn't explain or couldn't deny.

And I hated it.

"Why wouldn't I say that? It's the truth."

He shook his head before bringing his gaze back to me. "No. It's not. Everything we have is real. That stupid fucking bet doesn't matter."

"You don't get to decide that." I jerked away from him again, and this time I slipped from his grip. "You made that bet without a single thought about how I would feel. You didn't care that you made me look like a fool."

"Really?" He pushed his hands through his hair and pushed off the wall. "The only reason I said yes to that bet was because I give a shit about you. Do you really think I would do anything with Lucas if not? Do you think I would stoop to his level?"

"I didn't." I was honest with him because as much as I hated Carson at that moment, he still would never be anything like Lucas. "But you've proven to be exactly who you are again and again. You are not the boy who used to be my best friend."

"You're right." He swallowed so hard I could see the force of his Adam's apple pushing against his throat. "I am not him, and I will never be him again. Is that what you want? Do you want me to go back to that pathetic kid who didn't have a fucking clue about the world?"

His words were so harsh as he watched me, and they felt like a rough caress against my skin.

"I want you to go back to the guy who didn't need to be all this." I waved my hand in his direction. "I want you to go back to being the guy who wasn't more concerned with getting into girls' pants than he was with breaking their hearts."

"Is that all you think this was?" He laughed and a chill ran down my spine. "Me trying to get into your pants?"

"You succeeded. Didn't you?" I crossed my arms and stood my ground. My chest was heaving, and my heart raced, but I hoped he didn't notice either. I hoped he didn't see how affected I was by every little thing he said or did.

"I think I did more than succeed." He stepped closer to me, and I took a step back. My heels bumped into the baseboard before my back hit the wall. "I gave you more of myself than I've ever given to anyone else, Allie. If that doesn't mean anything to you, then fine, but it means something to me."

He searched my eyes, and I tried to calm down. "Because you kissed me?"

He laughed again and shook his head. "Because I kissed you, because I..." he hesitated, and I held my breath for his next words.

"What, Carson? What did you do?"

"I have been trying to hold myself back. I was dying every second that I was touching you to tell you that..." He hesitated again and searched my eyes. This time I let him. I let him have whatever time he needed to work out what was going on in that fucked-up head of his. "I love you, Allie."

His words should have thrilled me. I had been waiting for those words for as long as I could remember, but now they felt like a weapon.

Just another tool in his arsenal that he could use to destroy me.

Carson Hale didn't love me.

He had no idea what love was.

And it wasn't the idea of him not loving me that made me feel like I was breaking. It was the thought that I ever held onto any hope at all.

That sliver of hope that I tried to pretend wasn't there had been my downfall all along.

"Don't say things like that." My voice was far too shaky, and I hated that I allowed him to see that weakness.

"I mean it."

"No." I shook my head as the anger built inside me. "You don't. You don't ever mean the things you say."

"Allie, I don't know what you want me to say." He sounded just as frustrated as I did, but I didn't care. I could no longer be a doormat for him. I refused to be exactly like the rest of the girls he was used to running all over. Even if I had been exactly that up until this point. "What do you want me to do?"

"Leave me alone." I stared at him, and the ache in my chest became deeper. My words felt like a lie. They were a lie, but I knew that was what I needed. It didn't matter what I wanted from him. What I wanted and what I needed were as opposite as the two of us.

The things I wanted from him got me hurt. The things I needed did too, but it was different. It was the kind of hurt that I could protect myself with. The kind of hurt that I could use to make sure he wouldn't break my heart again in this lifetime.

"You don't mean that." He searched my face, and I knew I needed to get out of here. He looked so desperate, so scared of what I would say next, and I hated it. I hated that every part of me wanted to take that look away from him. I wanted to assure him that I would give him whatever he wanted from me.

But that was the problem.

If I didn't put distance between us, I would. I would give him everything, and he would take it.

And I would be left with nothing.

"I do." I moved to get past him, but he leaned into me, his body pressing against mine.

"I'm sorry." He choked out the words near my ear, and everything inside me felt like it was at war with itself.

I was so confused, so tired, and I didn't know how to answer him.

I didn't know how to stay away from him when everything made me feel like I was being pulled back.

"For what?" I turned my face to look at him, and our lips were so close to each other. His breath feathered against my lips as his chest rose and fell against mine, and even though I wanted to hate the feel of all of it, I didn't.

It felt like I was exactly where I was meant to be.

"For everything." He looked so hesitant as he spoke. "I'm sorry about the bet. I'm sorry that you think that what happened between us was fake. I'm sorry that I've been treating you like shit for a really long time."

"Carson." I shook my head.

"It's the truth. I've been a damn fool, and I'm sorry." He gripped my side in his hand, his fingers digging into me, and I didn't stop him.

"I don't forgive you."

His fingers tightened against me. "I don't expect you to."

"Then what do you expect? What do you want?" It was the question I was dying for him to answer and for him to finally give me some truth. I needed to know what he was going to take from me next, what I was going to give.

"I want you to forgive me even though you shouldn't. I want you to give me another chance." His voice was soft and like a caress over my skin.

"I can't." I looked away from him, but he reached out and caught my chin with his other hand.

"Please, Allie." His lips were pressed against my skin as

he spoke, and they broke through every barrier I had against him.

I couldn't just give him everything he wanted. I couldn't let him take everything I had to give, but I also couldn't walk away from him. Not in that moment when he was looking at me like I was the only thing that would take all his demons away.

He didn't deserve me, but I would give another piece of myself to him regardless.

I had no choice.

I didn't answer him because I knew he wouldn't like what I had to say. What I was giving him wasn't another chance, it was another moment. It was a moment that we both needed. A moment that I couldn't deny.

I turned to face him more, and I gently pressed my lips against his. He let out a harsh breath and his hands tightened against me.

He held me there for only a moment before his control seemed to snap and he buried his hand in my hair. His hold was painful, but I didn't want him to loosen it. My body begged for more.

His mouth slammed down against mine, and his kiss was frantic and wild. I could taste his hope on my lips and his desperation on my tongue. This was no longer a game to him. He wanted me as much as I had wanted him for years, and he was no longer the one who was in control.

Not really.

His teeth nipped against my bottom lip before he sucked it into his mouth, and I brought my hands to his shoulders to hold myself steady. As much as I wanted to hate him, my body still wanted him. I wanted everything I knew he could give me.

He kissed down my chin and along my jaw before moving to my neck. My hips jolted forward against his as his tongue tasted every inch of skin he passed. Every part of me felt like it was on edge, begging for his touch yet wholly unprepared.

"I need to taste you," he murmured against my skin before dropping to his knees in front of me.

He didn't wait for my answer before he lifted my shirt and pressed his mouth to my stomach. His tongue ran over my belly button as his fingers worked my shorts down my hips.

He was wasting no time. There were no pretenses about what either of us wanted. He ran his nose over the softness of my stomach before looking up at me. He didn't take his gaze away from mine as he pressed his mouth over my panties.

I tensed and bit down on my bottom lip. I was so ready, so desperate for him to give me more.

His fingers were spread wide as he pushed them up along my thighs, but they were so sure once they reached my panties. He jerked them down my legs until they fell to my feet with my shorts.

He was no longer looking up at me. He was staring straight ahead at my pussy, and I tried to breathe as I watched him.

I should have stopped him. Logically, I knew that, but I couldn't. I would face whatever consequences I had to face. I would deal with the heartbreak I knew I would feel when I walked out of here, but I just needed this rush he gave me.

If only for a moment, I needed to feel his hands on me and to pretend like nothing else mattered but the two of us.

It was a lie I was more than willing to believe for the

moment. A taste of his lies was far better than the truth. His lies were better than anything else I had ever experienced.

He slid his tongue against me before groaning. "God, you are so fucking wet."

I couldn't bring myself to be embarrassed. Instead, I lifted my foot and kicked off my clothes from around my ankles to give him better access to my body.

He lifted my thigh in his hand before I could get my foot back to the ground and put it over his shoulder. I was so open, so exposed in front of him, but he didn't lift his head away from my pussy for even a moment.

He dove into me. His mouth licking, sucking, and nipping at my flesh. I pushed even closer to him as I buried my hands in his hair. I was on my tiptoes with my head thrown back against the wall, and I felt like I was barely hanging on by a thread.

I could fall at any moment, and he would be the only thing I had to hold me up. He was the person I should have trusted least in the world, but I knew that even now that wasn't true.

"Carson," I called out his name because I already felt so close to an orgasm.

"You taste so good." His words vibrated against my pussy as his hand dug into my hip. "This pussy is mine, Allie. Do you hear me?"

I nodded even though we both knew what we were saying didn't really matter, but he growled at my answer. He lifted my other foot from the ground, gripping my thigh in his hand, and he rested it against his other shoulder.

I was in the air, my back against the wall, the weight of me resting on his shoulders, and he barely seemed to notice.

He ate me harder as his hands dug into my ass, tugging me closer to his mouth.

"Oh, God. Yes." I held on to him for dear life as I moved against him. I couldn't stop myself. My hips rolled against his face, and it only seemed to spur him on.

He sucked my clit into his mouth, and I slammed my head back against the wall. My orgasm rolled through me, the feeling racing through every corner of my body. Carson had complete control over me. I didn't know where I began and he ended. I didn't know how I was still leaning upright against the wall.

I could feel him moving beneath me before he pulled me away from the wall, and I grabbed onto his shoulders as he moved me down his body.

"Where are we going?" My voice was so sleepy and satisfied as he carried me.

"I need to get inside you," he growled against my neck. "I feel like I'm dying." He laid me down against the staircase. My ass hit the stairs before my shoulder blades pressed against the ones above it. Carson kneeled between my thighs, and he stared up at me as he quickly unbuttoned his jeans.

He paused just as he pulled out his cock, and he stared up at me. "We can't do this."

"What do you mean?" I leaned forward and wrapped my hand around him. He leaned forward into my touch, and I ran his cock against me. He slid through my wetness, back and forth from my clit to my opening, and I was dying for him to push inside me.

I had just come, but I wanted more. I was desperate to feel him inside me. I needed it.

"Allie." My name sounded painful on his lips. "I wasn't expecting this. I didn't bring a condom."

I heard what he said, but there was no rational thinking left in my brain. I didn't care about the stupid condom.

"Don't come inside me." I leaned back again and lifted my shirt to expose my stomach and breasts. "Come here." I ran my fingers over my skin and to my breast. I pinched my nipple between my fingers as he watched me.

"I've never." He shook his head. "I've never fucked anyone without a condom. I'm clean."

"Me neither." I smiled at him, and his lips tugged up on the side. I pinched my nipple again and I could feel the ricochet of my orgasm throughout my body. I tightened my thighs around Carson's hips before sliding my other hand down my body.

He was still watching me, and I couldn't take another second of it. I needed more. I slid my fingers over my clit and cried out at the feeling.

"Are you going to make me fuck myself?" I asked him before I thought better of it, and I could feel my embarrassment creeping in. I had never been so forward with Carson, with anyone.

"Fucking hell." Carson moved over me, and his mouth slammed against my mouth. He lined himself up before sliding into me with one long push. It felt so different than the last time, so much easier, but there was still a bite of pain.

"Oh, God." I wrapped my hand around the back of his neck as he began moving inside me.

He had one of my thighs in his hand, spreading me open for him, and he didn't stop kissing me. Not even for a moment.

My pussy clenched around him. I was still so sensitive from when he just ate me, and I already felt like I was on the brink of another orgasm.

"Nothing has ever felt this good." His words rushed out against my mouth, and even though I told myself not to believe him, every word felt like a shot to my chest. "This is what it should have always been."

Don't let him fuck with your head, Allie.

He lifted off me, moving to the stair at my side, and he grabbed for me. He pulled me over him until my thighs were straddling his, and he lowered me back down on him. He felt so much deeper like this.

I pushed my hands into his shoulders as I stared down at where we connected as I began to move. He gripped my ass in his hands and lifted me slightly before letting me fall back down against him.

Over and over, he helped me until I got the hang of the rhythm he set, then I took over. I rode him as he lifted my shirt and cupped my breasts in his hands. His fingers rolled over my nipples before his mouth pressed against the fabric of my bra.

The feel of him so deep inside me combined with the torturous gentleness of his mouth and hands was too much. I stared down at him as I rode him, and I didn't see the Carson who was capable of breaking my heart at every turn. I saw the Carson that I had fallen in love with a long time ago.

The one I couldn't seem to shake no matter how hard I tried.

I kept the pace as my heart thundered in my chest almost violently. He clung to me as if he was worried I would disappear at any moment, and I held him because I knew that fact to be true.

My orgasm coursed through my body, this one unbelievably stronger than the last, and I cried out his name. He didn't stop moving beneath me. He gripped my neck in his hand and forced my mouth down to meet his.

His kiss felt like a promise that I didn't believe, his hands a vow that I couldn't accept.

I tried to shield myself from both, but it was futile.

They flooded me without my permission. They suffocated me despite my armor.

"Oh, God, Allie." Carson's words were rushed and frantic, and I felt him come inside me only moments after I fell over the edge.

His arms were wrapped around me, and my forehead was pressed against his. I didn't have the courage to open my eyes yet or to utter a word. I just sat there and tried to calm my masochistic heart.

I could feel him shift beneath me, and the proof of the mistake we had just made leaked down my inner thighs. It was enough to make me come to my senses.

I climbed off of him before he could stop me, and I quickly grabbed my clothing from the ground. I glanced up at him long enough to see the panic in his eyes, but I didn't linger there. I couldn't.

"Allie." I heard him call my name, but I didn't stop. I finished getting dressed without even taking a moment to clean up, and I searched for my purse so I could leave.

"Baby. Please, stop."

I spun around to face him, and he was jerking his pants back up his hips. "I am not your baby."

I tried not to think about the look on his face as I walked away and made my way to the door. I could feel him following me, but I knew I couldn't stop. If I stopped for him, I knew I wouldn't be able to walk away.

"Please don't leave, Allie."

Every part of me wanted to turn around and stay, but I couldn't. I wouldn't survive him again. So, I did the one thing I knew he was the master of, I walked away.

CHAPTER 6

CARSON

I twisted the joint between my fingers as I tried to ignore my dad.

Apparently, Coach had called him about me getting benched, and I really wished he hadn't. My dad didn't give a shit. Not really. He just wanted to pretend he did. He just wanted something to be angry at.

Because he was always fucking angry.

"Are you done?" I looked up at him because I hadn't been listening for the last five minutes.

"Carson," my mother gasped my name, and I stared over at her. She looked worse than normal. Her hair was a complete mess and looked like she hadn't brushed it in days. She was in her robe even though it was only nine o'clock, and I wasn't sure if she had even changed out of it today.

"What, Mom?" I searched her face for a trace of the woman I loved, but it was so damn hard to find her anymore. "You can't seriously expect me to sit here and listen to him." I laughed before looking back to my dad.

"Aren't you a little lost anyway?"

"I am your father." His face was so red, and his fists were clenched at his sides.

That was always his answer. *I am your father*. As if that simple fact was supposed to mean something. He hadn't acted like much of a father in years.

He was nothing but a stranger.

"I can't deal with this." I tucked my joint behind my ear and stood from my chair. My mother's gaze bounced back and forth between me, and my father and immense guilt flooded me.

My mother couldn't choose between us. She refused to, even though he had given her every possible reason not to choose him.

When I looked at her, that was all I could see.

She had become the woman who would choose that asshole over her son and so much less like my actual mother.

"Mom. I'm going to head out." I could hear my dad still arguing behind me, but I completely blocked him out. He could rant all day about all the punishment and consequences for my actions, but he wouldn't stay here long enough to see any of it through.

All three of us knew that.

"Where are you going tonight?" She stared up at me and tucked her hair behind her ear.

"Just to Beck's." It was a lie. I was far too fucked up in the head right now to head back to Beck's. After everything that happened with Allie yesterday, and now dealing with my dad. I just needed to do *something*.

"I worry that you're there too much. I don't want you to impose on them." What she really didn't want was for me to leave her. I felt it in my soul, but she never said it. She wanted me to stay here and watch her waste away to nothing, but I couldn't do it.

I did it for so long, and I just couldn't anymore.

Because watching what he did to her, what he was still doing to her, it broke something inside of me that I couldn't fix.

"Don't worry, Mom. We stay out of Mr. and Mrs. Clermont's hair." I leaned down and kissed her on the forehead. I lingered there, taking in her familiar scent that filled me with nostalgia but also crushed me. She had always smelled like flowers, the kind that were wild and unkept and grew wherever they wanted, but now that was tainted with the strong smell of liquor on her tongue.

"I'll be back in the morning to check on you."

I didn't speak another word to either of them as I walked out of my house and out to my car. I had barely spoken to Olly or Beck today, and I had no idea what their plans were. I had no doubt that Beck was with Josie, and that meant Allie was probably nearby as well.

I sat in my driver's seat and bounced my leg as I stared down at my phone. Every part of me wanted to be with her. I wanted to call her right now and find out where she was so that I could find her. But I knew that wasn't what she wanted.

She hated me, probably more than I even realized, and yesterday did nothing to change that. If anything, it only made things worse.

I didn't want Allie to think that the only thing I wanted from her was sex, because it wasn't. Sex with her was amazing. I wouldn't deny that, but Allie was so much more than that. I had been an idiot for so damn long not to see it.

Where are you all at? I sent the text to Olly and Beck as I backed out of the driveway, and the reply from Olly was almost instant.

We're at the beach party. It's probably not a good idea for you to come.

I stared down at his message and was about to reply when his next message came through.

I'll come hang with you.

Fuck that. I pressed his name and lifted the phone to my ear.

He answered with a sigh. "Hey, man."

"Why shouldn't I come there?" I knew it had to do with Allie. Olly was the level-headed one, and I knew that he was just trying to protect her.

"Allie's been drinking. A lot, actually. I don't really think she wants to see you."

"Did she say that?" My heart pounded in my chest. Of course, she would say that. She had every right to, but I still hoped that she didn't. It was fucking irrational and stupid.

I had spent the last several weeks doing nothing but lying to her about that stupid bet, and now I expected something from her like she owed me anything. She didn't. Not a single thing, but I still wanted it.

It was so fucked up.

"Not exactly, but..." He trailed off, and I was about to scream before he finally spoke again. "She's had plenty to say about you in front of everyone."

I pulled out of my driveway and turned right toward the beach I knew they were at. I couldn't stop myself. If I was smart, I would have just gone back to Beck's and played a video game until they got home, or I would have called up some girl to make me forget all about Allie. But I wasn't smart.

"I'm headed that way."

Olly huffed, but me and him both knew it was going to happen. There was no way in hell I was going to leave Allie there drunk and not go and try to, fuck, I don't even know. Take care of her? Be around her? Just look at her for a damn second.

"Just don't show your ass. I'm not in the mood to clean up a fight tonight."

"I would never."

Olly chuckled at my words before hanging up the phone.

It didn't take me long to get to the beach. I could see the light of the bonfire from the road, and there were several cars parked along the edge of the sand and blocking my view.

I tucked my phone into the front pocket of my jeans as I climbed out of my car. It was cool tonight, and I was thankful I decided to wear my hoodie. I pulled the hood up around my head as I made my way down to the beach.

I spotted Josie and Frankie as soon as I passed the line of cars. They were both laughing with a drink in their hands, but I didn't see Allie. I headed toward them as I searched the crowd for her. Then I saw her sitting down in the sand with the biggest grin on her face.

I walked up next to Beck and Olly, but Allie didn't notice me. She leaned her head back and stared up at the night sky while her curls whipped around her face in the ocean breeze. She was so damn beautiful, and she looked so happy.

I watched her, the smile on her face not fading for a second, and I knew that it was a mistake for me to come here. I should have let her have this moment, this night, to herself without me ruining everything for her.

I took a step back, and Olly cocked his head to stare at

me. I nodded to the car before lifting my chin in his direction, then slowly turned and started making my way up the beach.

I was such an idiot. Moments like this, when I saw how happy she was when I wasn't around, these were the moments that fucked with my head the most. Being with me didn't make Allie happy. If anything, I hurt her more than not.

And I couldn't do that to her regardless of how much I wanted the opposite to be true.

I had made it about five steps away when I heard my name pass her lips.

"Are you really just walking away like none of us saw you standing there?"

I looked over my shoulder, and she had one eye winked open to look at me.

"You seemed to be enjoying yourself." I shrugged just as she closed both of her eyes.

"I was. I still am." She patted the sand next to her. "Come sit with me."

Both Frankie and Josie were eyeing me as I passed by them, but I gave them the biggest smile I could muster. Josie rolled her eyes, and a genuine smile ghosted upon my lips.

I sat down in the sand next to Allie, leaving a good foot between us, and she turned to look at me. "Where have you been?"

"With my parents." I searched her face as she stared at me. "Getting my ass reamed for getting benched."

"Well, you wouldn't be benched if you didn't get into a fight," she said it like that idea hadn't occurred to me.

"I wouldn't have gotten into a fight if you hadn't decided to date the douchiest guy in the entire country."

She finally blinked both eyes open and looked at me. "Are you trying to say that you being so territorial over me is my fault?"

"No." I shook my head even though I guess I kind of was. "I'm just saying that you decided to go out with the biggest asshole who makes comments about you that I can't fucking stand. If he tells anyone else that he's slept with you..."

She moved closer to me, and the scent of her perfume overwhelmed me. "What will you do?"

"I'll fucking kill him."

She grinned at my words and the growl in my voice, and her gaze didn't waver from my mouth. "You're really hot when you get jealous. Did you know that?"

I looked up at our friends who were all pretending not to be listening in on our conversation, but I knew that they all were. I looked back at Allie and adjusted my jeans. If she didn't stop staring at me like that, I wasn't going to care who was around us. "How much have you had to drink?"

"A little bit." She pinched her thumb and finger together to show me the slightest amount of space.

"I think you've maybe had a bit more than that."

Her hand dug into the sand as she leaned even closer to me. It was as if her body was doing it all on its own without her permission.

"Maybe." She shrugged and brought her eyes up to meet mine. "We should go swimming."

She was out of her mind. It was cold enough just sitting out here on the beach. The ocean would be freezing tonight.

"Not happening." I shook my head and moved a rogue curl out of her face.

"You know that you don't get to tell me what to do,

right?" Her hand inched closer to mine in the sand, and when they finally met, I felt the touch straight to my cock.

"You're freezing." Her hand felt like ice, and I finally looked down at what she was wearing. A pair of blue jean shorts covered her ass and not much more, and a small t-shirt that barely met the fabric of her jeans.

"I'm fine."

I leaned forward and reached behind my head, pulling my sweatshirt off in one long tug, and I pushed it in her direction. Her cheeks were flushed as she took it.

She didn't hesitate as she pulled her arms through the sleeves and then the rest over her head. It swallowed her whole, my sweatshirt at least three times too big for her, and God, she looked so adorable in it.

She brought the front of my sweatshirt to her nose, and she closed her eyes are she breathed heavily. "You smell so good." Her voice was dreamy and full of lust, and I had no idea how much she actually had to drink, but I knew that she wouldn't have said that out loud if she was thinking clearly.

Josie grinned down at her friend before linking her arm with Frankie's. "Allie, we're going to get another drink. Do you want to come with us, or do you want to stay with Carson?"

I wanted to kill her because I didn't want Allie to move an inch unless it was closer to me.

"I'll stay with him."

Josie raised an eyebrow in my direction, and I rolled my eyes. "I've got her."

"Uh-huh," she mumbled, but still walked away with Frankie on her arm. Beck and Olly followed behind them like two lovesick puppies, and I turned to look back at Allie once we were finally alone.

"Do you think that Olly likes Frankie?" She was squinting as she stared at them walking away from us, and even drunk, I was sure she noticed the way Frankie looked back over her shoulder and shared a smile with Olly.

"I don't know." I rubbed the back of my head because I didn't know how to answer her. "I think it's complicated."

"Oh God." She groaned and rolled her eyes before standing.

"What?" I climbed to my feet and put a steadying hand on her elbow.

"You and all are your complications." She did air quotes with her fingers as she said the last word. "If you like a girl, just say it. It's really not that hard."

"Okay." I smirked because she was so damn cute, especially when she was flustered. "I like you, Allie."

"Oh, dear God." She rolled her eyes even harder before walking away from me.

I followed behind her step for step and finally caught up enough to look down at her face. "What? I'm not allowed to like you?"

She stopped in her tracks and poked her finger into my face. "No. You're allowed to, but you don't. What you like is a girl who is willing to get on her knees for you without any other complications." She air quoted her fingers again before continuing her walk.

I had no idea where she was going, but she was leading us away from the party and further down the beach. The further she moved from the bonfire, the darker it got, and the urge to pick her up and carry her back was overwhelming.

"Considering you've never gotten on your knees for me, and I still like you, I think that proves your little theory wrong."

She swirled on me again, this time pressing her chest to mine, and I felt like I was the one who now needed to be steadied. "I would, though, and that's the point."

"You would what?" I swallowed as I watched her search my face. My heart hammered in my chest and my stupid cock strained against my jeans. She was barely even touching me, and already I felt like she was torturing me.

"I would get on my knees for you."

I groaned at her words and ran my fingers through my hair. She stared at my mouth before meeting my eyes, and I knew that I could get lost in her forever. "Don't say shit like that."

"Why not?" She pushed her hair out of her face and her tongue just barely ran over her bottom lip. "It's the truth."

"You don't even like me, remember?" I gripped her upper arm in my hand to keep some separation between us because I felt like I was falling into her.

"I don't have to like you to want to taste you."

My cock jumped at her words, and I cursed as I watched her. "You're drunk."

She rolled her eyes again and wrapped her fingers into my t-shirt. "I haven't had that much to drink."

"You hated me yesterday."

"I still hate you." She pushed even closer and everywhere she touched me felt like a brand. "But I'm clearly a sucker for punishment. I'm willing to ruin myself over and over for you."

"God, Allie." I stepped back, and she stumbled forward at my sudden movement.

"What?" She reached out for me and steadied herself with her hand on my forearm.

"Don't say shit like that."

"Why not? It's the truth." She blinked up at me, and I hated that I made her believe that. I was solely responsible for this girl believing that the shit I had given her was what she deserved.

"Is that what you think I want from you? For you to be hurt by me over and over?" I didn't. Of course, I didn't.

She raised her chin and stared at me. "Yes, Carson. I do. That's what you've proven to me. That's what you've slammed in my face."

"Fuck." I shook my head and looked back at the party before looking at her again. "It's not." I thought carefully about the next words I said to her because I needed her to know that they were the truth. Regardless of everything else that happened between us, this was the truth. "I know that I'm fucked up. I know that better than anyone, and I also know that I've taken my fucked-up shit out on you."

She pulled her gaze away from mine, but I lifted my hand and touched her jaw until she was forced to see me again. "I am sorry for what I've done. I'm sorry that I fucked up our friendship with my own family bullshit. I'm sorry that I was so damn cruel to you all these years because I couldn't physically stand to watch you, and I'm sorry for everything that happened with Eli and that fucking bet."

She shook her head rapidly as if she was trying to convince herself not to believe me.

"I didn't mean for you to get hurt, especially after—"

"After what?" Her harsh voice interrupted me.

"After everything that happened between us. I care about you, Allie."

"I can't." She looked up at me, and I saw the shift in her eyes. She didn't want to hear my words or apologies. They didn't matter to her. Not now, maybe not ever. "I'm not trying to be your girlfriend, Carson. I'm trying to get off. Can you do that, or should I find someone else?"

My temper flared, and I watched every small movement of her body as I tried to calm myself down. She dropped her hand from my skin and turned to head back to the party, but I grabbed her hand in mine before she could move out of my reach.

I jerked her backward until her back hit my chest and the small moan that left her mouth was like fuel to my anger and lust. I wanted to fuck her right there in the sand to prove to anyone who could possibly see us that this girl belonged to me. It didn't matter that she didn't believe it.

She was mine, and she had been for a long damn time.

And if what she wanted, needed from me, was to give her a simple fucking release, then I would do that for her. I knew that she wouldn't hate me any less tomorrow. Hell, she might even hate me more, but I refused to let anyone else touch her. Not when she came to me first.

If Allie was going to allow me to touch her, then I was going to take it. I would take any and everything she would give me at this point, even if that meant she would still walk away from me at the end of it.

I pressed my hand into her stomach, and I felt it tremble beneath my touch. "What do you want, Allie?" I breathed against her neck before I traced her chill bumps with my tongue.

She groaned but didn't answer me.

I nipped her earlobe with my teeth, and she pressed her ass back against my erection. I couldn't stop the deep groan that left my mouth or the way my hand tightened on her skin to force her even closer. "Tell me. What do you want?"

"You." Her voice was breathless and small, and I hated it.

"No, baby," I whispered against her ear, and she shuddered against me. "I need more than that. Tell me exactly what you want or I'm not touching you."

She raised her chin defiantly to face me. "I can find somebody else."

My grip became so tight against her. "No one else is fucking touching you." I ran my nose along her jaw, and she swayed against me. "I'll kill anyone who tries."

"I'm not yours." There was no conviction to her voice. Not even she believed what she was saying.

"We both know that's a lie." I snaked my hand under the edge of my sweatshirt and toyed with the bare skin of her stomach just above her shorts. "Don't we?"

She leaned her head back and shook her head against my shoulder, and her hips chased the movement of my hand.

"Tell me this is mine." I sank my fingers lower and cupped her pussy over her shorts. "Tell me who this belongs to, and I'll give you whatever you want."

"Oh God," she cried out as I pressed my hand firmer against her. "It's yours. Please, it's yours."

I buried my hand beneath her shorts and panties, and I groaned deep and heavy when her arousal coated my hand. "You're so fucking wet for me." I lapped at the base of her neck as I moved my palm against her clit. She moaned, but I didn't give her any time before I pushed a finger inside her. She was so damn tight, but I still entered a second as she rolled her hips against my hand.

"I want to feel you." She lifted her arm and wrapped it

behind my neck, and I used my free hand to cup her breast through my sweatshirt as she tugged me tighter against her.

No one could see us where we stood, but we could still see them. Their laughter was like an echo that mingled with the crashing waves of the ocean and the harsh pulls of our rushed breaths.

It didn't matter either way. They could all be watching us, and I wouldn't be able to pull away from her. The only one that would be able to stop me was her, and I prayed that she didn't.

Her legs trembled against mine, and I pulled her harder against my body so she would use me as support as she let go. She reached behind her and forced her hand between our bodies until her touch skated over my cock. I groaned against her skin and moved my hand faster against her.

This was what I had become. Once upon a time, I would barely even notice when a girl would touch me in such an innocent way, but it felt so fucking erotic with her. Her skin wasn't even touching mine, and already, I felt like I was going to lose myself to her.

"I want to taste you." She looked back at me, and I brought my lips down against hers. I kissed her until she whimpered against my mouth, but she shook her head. "No." Her hand tightened over my cock. "I want to taste you here."

"Fuck." I pumped my fingers harder inside her and curved them forward until she was pushing to her tiptoes to chase the movement. "Not tonight. I don't want you to regret it."

"I won't." She kissed my chin before moving along my jaw. "I think about it all the time. I know that I won't be as good as what you're used to, but..."

"Goddamn it." I pulled my hand from her shorts and grabbed her hand in mine before tugging her behind me. There was almost nowhere on the beach that provided any sort of real privacy, but I had to find something.

We moved farther down the beach and I stopped when we got far enough away that I could no longer hear anything but the pounding of my own heart.

I ran my fingers through her hair and nipped her bottom lip into my mouth. She moaned, the sound being swept away in the breeze, before she dropped to her knees in front of me.

Her hands trembled as they moved to my pants, and I could barely stand to watch her.

Allie on her knees before me was a sight that felt too provocative to bear.

She was the most alluring dream and a bewitching nightmare. She was everything I had ever wanted and the one thing I couldn't endure.

She managed to undo the button of my jeans before she unzipped my zipper. I jumped at the feel of her soft hand against my stomach, and she searched my eyes as she tugged my jeans and boxers down my hips only far enough to give her access.

She ran her tongue over her lips as she stared at my cock, and I almost died. I buried my hands in her hair and stared up at the night sky in an attempt to calm myself down.

Her small hand wrapped around my cock, and she moved it up and down until I felt my cock hit her lips.

"Fuck." My gaze dropped down to hers, and she was still staring up at me as she teased her tongue out of her mouth and ran it along the tip.

She may have thought she wouldn't have been as good at

this as the others I've had before, but she was dead fucking wrong. She had barely touched me, and I felt like I was suffocating. I was drowning in her, and I didn't know how to stop. Nothing I did or said would bring me up for air.

She flattened her tongue against me before lowering her mouth around me, and she didn't stop until her mouth hit her fist.

I was so careful not to tighten my hands in her hair or to force her down further or harder. I just wanted whatever she was willing to give me. I was about to come just thinking about the fact that I was the first person she had ever done this with, and I never wanted to think about her doing it with anyone else.

I never wanted to give anyone else a single opportunity to touch her ever again.

She pressed her hand into my thigh and held on as she moved against me. Her other hand continued to work me at the base of my cock, and she slammed her mouth against it with every meeting pass.

"You are so fucking good at this."

Her eyes snapped back up to mine, and she hummed her approval at my words. The vibration of her mouth shot straight to my balls, and I knew that I was going to come before she had a chance to even explore me.

My stomach tightened, my lower back ached with the urgency to let go, but I wrapped my fingers in her hair harder and I rubbed my thumb over her cheek as I watched her eagerly taste me.

"Allie, baby." I tightened my fingers in her hair and forced her to bring her eyes back up to me. "I'm going to come in your mouth if you don't stop."

This time she let out a deep groan and her hand left my

thigh before I watched it sink beneath her shorts. She didn't take her eyes off me as her hand began to move against her pussy. I was so shocked by this girl who seems so innocent.

I had never been so turned on in all my life. I was jealous of those two fucking fingers that were taking everything that I wanted from her.

I couldn't stand still as I watched her mouth sucking me and her hand fucking her. I began to move, pumping in and out of her mouth, and she let me. She opened her mouth wider and flattened her tongue, and her hand moved faster and faster the harder I slammed into her mouth.

She was right there with me. I could tell by the way her eyes turned molten and her body became stiff beneath my hands. We were going to come together on this beach with no fucking cares about who could see us or what they thought.

Her perfect mouth and that tiny little hand were going to be the end of me, and I didn't know what I was going to do when she no longer wanted this from me. When she no longer wanted to use her drunkenness as an excuse to touch me because she was too afraid to just say that she wanted me.

She needed that excuse. She needed something to blame when she regretted me tomorrow, and I would let her have it.

She cried out around me, her mouth tightening around my cock, and I didn't stand a chance as I watched her come against her fingers and I came in her mouth.

Her eyes widened as I hit along the back of her throat, but she didn't hesitate as she swallowed everything that I gave her. She stared up at me with a look that was liable to split me right in half, but I didn't know what she was looking for.

I loosened my hands in her hair and rubbed my fingers over her cheeks as I pulled out of her mouth, and I was at risk of coming again when I watched her run the tip of her thumb along her bottom lip to gather the small amount of spit and traces of me that had escaped her.

I gripped her beneath her arms and lifted her until she was standing in front of me again, and I heard my name barely pass her lips before I pressed mine against hers. I could already feel her hesitation and her regret, and I was desperate to kiss her until she forgot about both.

She could lie all she wanted and say that this was only about sex for her, but we both knew that was a lie. It had always been more for us. Always.

I just had to make her remember why that more was worth it.

CHAPTER 7
ALLIE

When I woke up this morning, regret hit me like a ton of bricks, and it wasn't regret over what I had done. I couldn't pretend like I regretted a second of that.

Because I didn't.

But it was everything else. It was how I knew that I had looked at him and the shit I said that I never would have if I hadn't been drinking. I regretted that I had let my defenses down around him when I had promised myself that I wouldn't.

Carson hadn't let me out of his sight after he kissed me senseless. Instead, he stayed so close to me that I think he feared I would disappear at any moment or simply remember why I shouldn't want to be around him.

He kept sneaking fleeting touches and longing glances, and even though I had been drinking, it messed with my head. It messed with it when he made sure I got back to Beck's house and in Josie's bed in one piece, and it continued to mess with it when I woke up this morning with a pounding headache.

"How are you feeling?" Josie walked into the room and handed me a bottle of water. She was wrapped in a towel from the shower, and she looked like she felt so much better than I did.

"Okay." I groaned and pressed the cold bottle to my forehead.

She chuckled as the bed dipped, and she leaned back against my legs. "You don't sound like you feel okay."

"How badly did I embarrass myself last night?"

She pulled my hand down away from my face so she could see my eyes. "You didn't. Do you not remember last night?"

"Oh. I remember it." I groaned again. "I'm pretty sure I looked like a lovesick puppy for a guy that everyone had just watched use me for a bet."

"You did not." She laid down beside me and turned on her side to stare at me. "And I know that you're pissed at Carson. I'm pissed at him too, but I think he actually cares about you."

"I think he's just enjoying the fact that even though I'm pissed at him, I still can't keep my hands to myself."

Josie chuckled, and I rolled my eyes. "I don't think it's that at all, but I did notice that the two of you disappeared down the beach. What happened there?"

"You don't want to know." I closed my eyes in an attempt to block the memories, but it was a mistake. He was all I could think about. Memories of the night before flooded me. The way he felt, the way he tasted, the way he had looked down at me when I was in control of his pleasure.

"I absolutely want to know." She nudged my knee with hers. "I'm trying to live vicariously through you."

"What?" I opened my eyes and stared at her like she was

crazy. "You have Beck. Why would you ever want to live vicariously through me?"

"I don't mean it like that. I just remember what the hate sex was like. You know?" She wagged her eyebrows at me. "I try to start a fight at least once a week."

"You're insane." I chuckled and sat up in bed to down the water she had brought me.

"Probably, but don't think that's going to get you out of giving me details."

I stood from the bed and stretched, and it was at that moment that I realized I was wearing nothing but Carson's sweatshirt and my panties.

My gaze jerked to Josie, and she grinned. "You had your pants off before Carson even left the room, but he walked out before you removed the rest."

"Oh my God." I pressed my hand to my face. "Who put the sweatshirt back on me?"

"That was me because you demanded it. Apparently, you wanted to go to sleep smelling like Carson."

By the look on her face, I knew that it was as embarrassing as it sounded. "I'm never going to show my face again. This is it. I have to move."

"Don't be so dramatic." She waved me off like embarrassing myself in front of Carson wasn't my idea of a personal hell. "Plus, he's still here. The boys and Frankie are swimming in the pool, so you're going to have to face him before you can even get home to pack your things."

"Fuck." I didn't want to face him. I didn't want him to look at me and remember me on my knees in front of him like I had never been so desperate for something in all my life. "I cannot face him today."

"Yes. You can." She climbed from her bed and moved to

her dresser. She threw a hot pink bikini onto the bed, then pointed at me. "Go put your ass in that right now and clean your face. Once you're put together, we will go out there, and we will pretend like last night was so unmemorable that you haven't even thought about it once."

"We both know that's a lie."

"That doesn't matter." She pulled her own bathing suit out and stared at me. "We won't let him see that. You can be whoever you want to be, Allie, and that includes with men. If you don't want Carson to think that you called out his name in your dream last night, then you make sure that he doesn't."

"That did not happen."

"Oh, but it did." She pointed to the bathroom for me to get a move on. "That's why I'm so interested in the details of what happened on the beach because it sounded good."

I grabbed the bathing suit from the bed and headed to the bathroom before she could tell me anything else about what I did last night that I would regret. "It's not going to happen."

"Don't make me ask Carson!" she yelled after me, but I closed the door before answering her back.

I changed into the bathing suit before piling my hair onto the top of my head and washing my face. I grabbed my toothbrush from Josie's toothbrush holder, and I stared at myself in the mirror.

I looked far too eager and too happy to know that Carson was still here. I needed to rein myself in. He freaking hurt me, and here I stood looking like the love of my life was outside waiting on me.

Get your shit together, Allie.

I finished brushing my teeth and pushed out of the bathroom. Josie was sitting on the end of the bed with a smile on her face, and I rolled my eyes as I passed by her and grabbed the towel she was holding out to me.

I didn't stop or hesitate as I snatched a pair of Josie's sunglasses and pushed my way out the door. There was no way that I was going to let him know how affected I was by him. I refused to allow him to think that he had somehow managed to get under my skin.

It didn't matter if he actually had.

It was inconsequential that it was where he lived.

He didn't need to know that.

As soon as the sun hit my skin, I felt his eyes on me. I didn't look in his direction as I walked over to the lounge chair and straightened my towel out. It didn't matter, though. I could pretend all I wanted, and I could act as unfazed as I would never feel, but he would still have such an effect on me.

I turned in his direction and sat down on the end of the lounger just as Josie sat down next to me.

"Are you coming in?" Frankie asked before swimming to the edge of the pool right in front of us.

"Yeah. We're coming."

"How did you sleep?" She shielded her eyes from the sun and stared straight up at me.

"Like a rock."

Josie snorted, and I kicked my foot against hers.

"You should have since you were in my spot." Beck pouted from where he swam. "I can't believe you made me go back to my room last night."

"You're fine." Josie rolled her eyes and stood. She jumped into the pool right next to Beck, and he laughed as she swam to the surface and immediately wrapped her arms around his neck.

I could still feel Carson watching me, and I finally looked over to meet his gaze. He was more than watching me. He was staring at me with a look so intense that I had no idea what it meant. I wasn't sure if it was hate or lust or some mixture of things I couldn't put my finger on.

But I was so fucking mesmerized by that stare that I didn't even realize that Frankie was still talking to me.

"Allie?"

"Huh?" I pulled my gaze away from him and looked down at my friend.

She cocked her head and looked at me with a smile on her face. "I was just saying that we were going to order pizza for lunch. Are you cool with that?"

"Oh, yeah. Of course." I stood and walked to the opposite end of the pool, as far from Carson as I could possibly get, and walked into the warm water. It was cool outside, typically too cool to be swimming when you were sane, but the Clermonts left their pool open year-round because that kind of money meant heated pools and all sorts of other luxuries.

I sank down into the water until it teased the tops of my shoulders and sagged into the warmth.

"How are you feeling today?" Olly cocked his head and grinned at me.

"I have a bit of a headache, but I'm fine."

"That's good." He glanced over his shoulder to where Carson was swimming in our direction, and I tried to hide the way my body tensed. "I figured you'd be a little worse for wear after the amount of alcohol you consumed."

"I probably should feel worse." I messed with my hair

and tried to look anywhere but at Carson. He was only a handful of feet away from me now.

"I made her take a few Tylenols and chug some water before she went to sleep last night." His gruff voice sent shivers down my spine, and as soon as he said the words, memories of last night flashed before my eyes.

He had done as he said even though I didn't want to do either. All I had wanted was him. I had practically begged him to stay and sleep in Josie's bed with me.

But he had refused.

"Thank you for that." I forced out the words and ran my fingers through the water. "I don't think I was thinking very clearly last night."

He grinned like he knew better, and so did I. I may have been drinking, but I didn't ask Carson for anything last night that I hadn't wanted. I wanted it then and I would still want it now. The only difference was that the alcohol had made me braver. It had taken away my self-preservation and only focused on the part of me that still looked at Carson like he was the best thing to ever happen to me.

I was an idiot.

"You're welcome." He moved even closer to me in the water, and my stomach tightened. I wondered if he was thinking about what had happened between us last night. I obsessed over the thoughts of him in my mouth while I got myself off with my hand.

I was desperate to know if it had felt the same to him, if he had been more turned on than he ever had before, or if it was lackluster in comparison to what he had before. I hated that I did that. I hated that I compared myself, but I wasn't an idiot.

Carson was far from innocent, and even though he was

the first guy I had even gotten on my knees for, I knew that there had been a long line of girls in front of me who had been willing to do it for him.

"I think you were thinking clearer than ever last night."

My gaze snapped to him. How did he get so close?

"You would like to think that."

Olly snorted out a laugh just as I felt Carson's hand touch mine. I tried to jerk away, but he didn't allow it. Instead, he pulled me closer to him until my legs pushed against his underwater. I forced my other hand between us and pressed against his chest to give me some space.

"You would like to think that I'll believe anything you said last night was a lie when we both know that isn't true."

I turned in Olly's direction, but he already had his back turned to us and was now talking to Frankie.

"I don't remember saying anything." I lied, and the way he stared down at me told me that we both knew it.

"Do you not remember anything from last night?" He raised an eyebrow and pushed his fingers until they linked with mine. "If you'd like for me to remind you." He leaned forward and pressed his other fingers to my lips. Water dripped from his fingers onto my skin, and I couldn't help myself as I peeked my tongue out just enough to taste it.

His gaze was glued to my mouth as he spoke his next words. "That mouth of yours did far more than spill your secrets last night."

"I don't need to be reminded." I straightened my spine. "I know exactly what my mouth did and didn't do."

His smile cocked up on the side and the tiniest little dimple appeared on his cheek. If we were anywhere else, if we were anyone else, I would have leaned forward and traced the dip of his skin with my tongue, but we weren't. I wasn't supposed to be turned on by that small little feature that I hadn't seen on his face in what felt like years.

He was supposed to be the guy that I still hated.

I had no other choice if I wanted to protect myself. I had already given him far too many chances, and he had fucked every one of them up. He had taken advantage of every bit of kindness I had extended to him, and I knew that was all he was capable of.

So it didn't explain why I still felt desperate to lean into him and pretend like none of our past ever existed. This was me and him, and I knew us better than anyone. I knew exactly what we were and what we would never be, but it didn't matter.

My head was still clouded by the idea of what I wanted and not what I could have.

"Do you?" He sank down into the water and tugged me forward until I had no choice but to catch myself with my hands on his chest. He took the opportunity to wrap his arms around me and pull me even tighter.

"What are you doing?" I whispered and looked to our friends. Every single one of them were watching us even though they were pretending like they weren't.

"What?" One of his hands skimmed my thigh and he attempted to raise it enough to wrap around his waist. I desperately wanted to. I wanted to fall into him and pretend like it was exactly where I was meant to be. But I couldn't. I stiffened my leg in his touch and refused to move any closer. "You can give me the best head of my life, but I'm not allowed to touch you the next morning?"

"Don't do that." I shook my head and tried to push away from him, but his hold on me didn't budge.

"Do what?" He was staring down at my mouth again, and

I was dying to know exactly what was going through his head.

"Don't act like you haven't been with half of this damn town." The words tasted like ash in my mouth. I hated them. I despised them. "I don't need you to give me any fake-ass" —I waved my hand in his direction— "whatever that was."

He grinned even harder, and I no longer wanted to kiss it. I wanted to smack that look right off his face. "You are too damn smart to be that dumb."

"Did you really just call me dumb?"

"I did." He nodded his head then tightened his hands around me when I tried to pull away. "It's dumb of you to think that anyone else I've ever been with comes close to comparing to you." He moved even closer to me, and his lips pressed against my ear as he spoke. "No one has ever come close to even comparing to what I dreamed being with you would be like, but now that I know?" His head shook next to mine. "I'll never be sated by anything but the taste of you ever again."

My heart felt like a caged animal dying to break loose as I turned my head to look at him. There wasn't a trace of pretense or uncertainty in his eyes. Whether what he said was true or not, he believed it, and I had never wanted to kiss him more.

I leaned closer to him, my body doing for me what my head refused, and I stared at his mouth. This felt different. This wasn't a drunken hook-up or a moment I could blame on anger. I simply wanted him, and it felt far more dangerous than anything else.

Wanting him had been my downfall for far too long.

"Allie," he whispered my name, and I didn't know if it

was a question or if he was trying to tell me something, but I knew that I loved the way it sounded coming from his lips.

His gaze raked over me, roaming from my mouth to far beyond the water's edge, and he looked like he was starved.

When he looked at me like that, I felt like nothing and no one could touch us. It felt like we were lost in our own little world, a world that belonged to only us, and I never wanted to leave it. Leaving that bubble we created was where I got in trouble, it was when I got hurt.

"Olly!" Frankie's scream broke the moment between us just before she hit the water and her splash drenched us both. I laughed as I pushed away from him and tried to put some distance between us.

Carson was still watching me, and I knew that he wanted to say something. I could see the look in his eyes and the stiffness in his jaw, but I wasn't ready to hear whatever it was he wanted to say.

I couldn't handle it right now. Not emotionally and especially not in front of our friends.

I shook my head, just the slightest bit, but he saw it. I knew because his eyes narrowed, and his jaw tightened further.

"I'm going to grab a drink," he said to no one in particular before jerking his gaze away from me and climbing out of the pool. I watched him, and there wasn't a single thing about his body that cooled the burning inside of me. If anything, it only made it worse.

Everything about him made things worse, and I closed my eyes and sank underneath the water to block it all.

CHAPTER 8

CARSON

Allie was going to be the death of me. There was no way around it.

All I could think about was her on her knees or her in that tiny pink bikini that left very little to the imagination. I also couldn't help thinking about how she seemed to want nothing other than me in one moment, then couldn't stand to look at me the next.

It was infuriating because I knew that she wanted me. She may not have liked me, but she wanted me just the same.

And I wanted her just as badly.

Our baseball game was already in the fifth inning, and I hadn't paid attention to a single second of it. I was sharing the bench with a sophomore who had just moved up to varsity but hadn't managed any game time yet, but I had barely spoken two words to him. Instead, I was bouncing my knee and thinking about how I thought Allie was going to kiss me last weekend.

She was so damn close, and the need was more than

evident in her eyes, but she pulled away. She pulled away and avoided me the rest of the damn day. Wherever I moved, she made sure to make an equal move in the opposite direction.

She was avoiding me, but she wouldn't be able to do it for long. We would be back at community service in just a couple of days, and she would have no choice but to talk to me.

"Did you see who's here?" Olly bumped my shoulder as he ran into the dugout and dropped his glove onto the bench.

I followed his gaze until I saw exactly who he was talking about. Allie was sitting in the front row of the bleachers with Josie and Frankie, and she was grinning like she had no concerns in the world. Like she wasn't driving herself crazy about me like I was about her.

"Of course, I saw her." I stared ahead at the field again. It was fitting that she had shown up to a damn game where I was still benched, where I looked like a pussy while Eli was out there smiling like the cocky piece of shit that he was. I knew that he had seen her too.

"She's looking over here at you."

I risked a glance in her direction, and he was right. Her gaze collided with mine for only a second before she quickly looked away, and I worried that I had imagined it all along.

"I have a feeling that she's not here to see me." I lifted my hat from my head before turning it backward and read-justing it.

"Bullshit." Olly looked over at the girls. "We both know that girl is crazy over you."

"That may have been true once upon a time, but she hates me right now."

"She doesn't hate you." He shook his head and opened his water. "You just need to do some more groveling."

"And you're the expert on relationships?" I cocked my eyebrow at him because we both knew the only relationship he wanted to be in was the most fucked-up situation of all.

"Of course not, but I'm not as fucking stupid as you and Beck. You two apparently think that fucking up in any way possible is the best way to get the girl." He rolled his eyes, and I chuckled.

"You have a point there."

"Shit." He stood from the bench so quickly that I looked around like I had missed something.

"What?"

"Your mom's here."

I heard his words, but they didn't fully register. My parents never came to my games. Never. They hadn't been to one in years, but when I looked back to where I had just been watching Allie, there stood my mother with a large purse on her shoulder and a plastic water bottle in her hand.

"Fuck," I cursed and moved to leave the dugout.

"What the hell do you think you're doing?" Coach pushed against my chest, and it took everything inside me not to knock him out of my way.

"My mom's here." I nodded in her direction, but he was still staring straight at me.

"And you can wait to go see her until after the game like the rest of the team."

I looked back to where she was standing and watched in horror as Allie stood and wrapped her arms around her neck. Of course, the two of them knew each other from when we were younger, but I didn't think they had seen each other in years.

"Goddamn it." I pushed through my teammates to get to the other end of the dugout where I could actually talk to my mom. "Hey, Mom. What are you doing here?"

She turned in my direction, and just from the smile on her face, I knew that she had been drinking. She was always drinking.

"I just thought I'd come to watch you play." Her smile widened. "I was watching from the car, but I didn't see you on the field."

"Coach suspended me for the week, remember?"

"Oh." Her face fell, and I knew that she didn't. She probably didn't remember a single moment from that night. "Silly me. I must have forgotten."

She smiled at me again before turning back to smile at Allie. Allie grinned back at her before her gaze fell to me, and I knew that she knew.

I could see the truth shining back at me from the pity in her eyes. It was pity that I fucking hated.

Even though Allie and I hadn't been friends in a long time, she knew what my mother had been through. She had been right by my side as things started to deteriorate. She was there until I pushed her away.

"You can sit with me if you want and still watch the game." Allie took my mom's hand in hers, and she let her. "I don't know a whole lot about baseball, but it's still pretty interesting even without Carson on the field."

My mom nodded before smiling at me, and she followed Allie to the bench.

Allie looked over at me as they sat down, and there was so much uncertainty and sympathy on her face. My chest tightened to the point of pain as I watched her. I loved my mother, but I didn't want Allie touched by the fucked-up mess my family was.

It didn't matter how well she knew her once upon a time. My mom wasn't the same person she had been then. She was nothing like her anymore.

I took a seat on the bench, right on the edge where I could watch them, and I tried to calm myself down. I had no idea why she was here, what made her decide to come today after not coming for years, but I had a sinking feeling in my stomach.

It was stupid, and I knew that, but I always felt on edge around both of my parents. My father was mostly because I knew exactly who he was. My mom, though, it was the unpredictability of who she had become that fucked with my head.

I didn't know what to expect with her or her drinking. Usually, she kept the severity of it locked up at the house. Those moments that she refused to let anyone else see, but I saw the way people looked at her. Even if they didn't know the truth about the demons she was battling, they had their suspicions.

"What's going on?" Beck sat down beside me, and Olly stood at his side blocking us from everyone else.

"Hell if I know." I looked over at them before looking at my mom. "But I know she's been drinking."

"Do you want me to ask Josie to take her home?"

"No." I shook my head. "I think I'm going to bounce and take her."

"Coach will have your ass." He gave me a warning that I didn't need. I already knew that I was beyond Coach's bad side.

"It looks like Allie is already handling it." Olly nodded in their direction, and I looked up to where they were sitting, except they were no longer there. Allie walked hand in hand with my mom, and they were laughing as they walked toward the parking lot.

"Shit." I grabbed my phone out of my bag to call Allie but noticed a text from her as soon as I turned it on.

I'm going to take your mom back to your house. Can you get her car?

Fuck. This was the last thing I wanted Allie to do or to see.

You don't have to do that. I'm coming.

I shoved my unused equipment into my bag and was about to lift it onto my shoulder when the next text came through.

We're fine. Finish your game and don't get your butt in trouble. I've got her. Promise.

My chest tightened even worse. It wasn't that I didn't trust her. I did. Far more than I would even like to admit, but I didn't trust what would happen or what Allie would see.

Are you sure?

This was stupid. Allie wasn't responsible for my mom. I was. It didn't matter what kind of trouble I would get into with Coach.

Yes. The game is almost over. You can meet her at your house when you're done.

I looked to the scoreboard, and she was right. We were at the top of the sixth inning, and the other team didn't stand a chance of catching up to us.

Fine. But you'll call me if you need me?

Of course.

I made sure my ringer was on before I sat my phone on

the back of the bench. If Coach found out it was on, he would be pissed, but I couldn't bring myself to care.

I sat back down and my leg bounced rapidly as I tried to calm myself down, but it didn't help. I continued to check my phone over and over, but I didn't have any messages from her. There were a few from some girls I never talked to anymore, but I quickly deleted those without responding.

It wasn't until the game ended that a text finally came through telling me that they had made it back to the house. I grabbed my shit before Coach could get a chance to stop me, and I headed straight for my mom's car.

I dropped to the ground and pulled out the hide-a-key I put there years ago before climbing inside and rushing to my house. I had no idea what state my mother was in, and I also didn't know how things were left between her and Allie.

I picked up my phone and dialed Allie's number, and I felt like I couldn't catch my breath as I waited for her to answer.

"This is Allie. I can't get to the phone..."

I hung up and threw my phone down in the passenger seat.

CHAPTER 9
ALLIE

I poured Mrs. Hale another cup of coffee before taking my seat beside her again at the island.

"Thank you." She smiled up at me, and I could finally see some flashes of the woman I used to know behind the strong smell of liquor and her trembling hands.

"So, what are your plans after high school?"

"Oh." I tucked some curls behind my ear. "I'm going to still work at the country club and go to Clermont Bay Community College."

Her smile was weak, but it was genuine. "I bet your parents are happy to have you sticking around here."

"They are." I nodded, but my leaving had never even crossed any of our minds. Moving out of state meant out-of-state tuition, and there was no way we could possibly afford that. "Plus, I'm going to try to live in my bedroom until they force me out."

Mrs. Hale laughed before taking a long sip of her coffee. "Trust me when I tell you that I doubt that will ever happen.

Mamas want their babies to stay babies for as long as they can."

"What about you?" I asked, genuinely interested in getting information on Carson. "Are you ready for Carson to head to college?"

"No and yes." She shook her head no even through her answer. "I'm ready for him to explore the world and figure out who he is without us." She waved her hand around the house. "But I'm also not ready to have him out of my sight."

"I don't blame you." I didn't mean it the way that it sounded, but when Mrs. Hale gave me a giant smile, I couldn't help the blush that crept up my face.

"I didn't mean it like that." I stumbled over my words. "I mean, yes. He is nice to look at, but I just meant that I'm sure it's nice to have him around all the time."

His mom chuckled and ran her fingers over her cheek. "You don't have to be embarrassed. You both used to have the biggest crush on each other when you were kids. I wondered if it had continued."

"It hasn't." I shook my head, and the lie tasted bitter on my tongue. "Your son doesn't have crushes."

"That's what he'd like you to believe." She stood from her stool, and even though she tried to hide it, it was blatantly obvious when she pulled a bottle of clear liquid from the counter and poured some into her cup. "Carson has always been good at keeping his feelings hidden."

I wanted to point out that his emotions might have been easier for her to read if she wasn't drinking, but I knew that wasn't fair. I didn't know anything about her anymore or what she had been through. What I did know was from the past, and it was very little.

I had no idea why she was still with Carson's dad, but I knew that I had no right to judge her.

"I don't know. Maybe you're right." I shrugged my shoulders. "I can't get a read on him at all most days."

"Can't get a read on who?" I jumped at the sound of Carson's voice. He moved around the corner, and he looked between his mom and me skeptically. He was still wearing his baseball uniform, and I knew that he had probably rushed here as soon as his game was over.

"Allie was just telling me about some boy in her school." His mom winked at me, and I couldn't stop the small snort that passed my lips.

"Uh-huh." His jaw tensed as he stared at me, but he moved toward his mom and pressed a kiss to her forehead. He spoke to her in hushed tones that I couldn't hear, and I watched as her eyes closed gently and a small smile formed on her lips.

I wondered if this was normal for them. If she was constantly drinking and he was constantly taking care of her. The thought hadn't even crossed my mind before tonight. I hadn't even considered what he was dealing with at home.

His mom brought her coffee cup to her mouth and drained the contents in one go. She was already so intoxicated, it was the reason I had decided to drive her home, but her hands were still shaking like she hadn't had enough.

"I need to get changed." Carson ran his fingers through his hair. "Allie, do you want me to walk you to your car?"

I tried not to let the slice of pain affect me. "No." I shook my head. "I'll stay until you're back."

He looked like he wanted to fight me on the subject, but he didn't. Instead, he shook his head and pushed past me and up to his room.

His mother looked from his retreating back to me. "I think I'm going to head to bed."

"Okay." I stood and moved around the island toward her. "Do you need help getting ready for the night? Do you need me to help you to bed?"

I knew that she probably hated me asking, but she still looked so unstable on her feet. She smiled at me before tucking the bottle of liquor underneath her arm and shaking her head. "No. I can handle it. Thank you, though, and thank you for driving me home."

"You're welcome."

"I don't know what got into me today." She ran her fingers over her chest and straightened her shirt. "I'm not usually like this."

"It's okay." I lied because even though I didn't think what she was doing to herself or Carson was okay, I wasn't here to judge her.

I tapped my fingers against the countertop as she walked past me and to her room, and part of me realized that I should have let Carson walk me out to my car. I hadn't wanted to leave her, but I was so out of my element here.

Once his mom rounded the corner and disappeared to her room, I grabbed my phone and keys off the counter and headed toward the door. I would simply text Carson and let him know that I was going to go ahead and head out and that his mom was in her room. He didn't need me here any longer, and I had no interest in facing him and any questions he may have had.

I had just reached the door when I heard him coming back down the stairs. My heart hammered in my chest, and I hadn't even turned in his direction.

"I thought you were going to stick around?"

I turned around to face him and watched as he ran his fingers through his hair. He was so damn handsome, and even though I knew that fact, it still hit me like a ton of bricks every time I saw him.

"Your mom is going to bed." I pushed my phone into my back pocket because the need to fidget was overwhelming. "I just wanted to make sure she got settled in."

"What about me?" He was searching my eyes, but I didn't know what he was looking for. There were so many things he would find there, but I didn't think any of them were something that he wanted to face tonight. "Did you not want to make sure that I was settled in?"

I rolled my eyes. "You're a big boy, I think you can take care of yourself." He raised an eyebrow, and I realized my mistake. "That is not what I meant."

He took a few steps closer to me, and I swear my body was acutely aware of every inch he closed between us. "I didn't say anything."

"I know exactly what you are thinking."

"And how is that?" He was only a step away from me now, his body within arm's reach, and we both knew it. It felt like there was a string between us that was pulled so taut that it could snap at any moment. "You just assume you know what I'm thinking all the time, but you have no idea."

I rolled my eyes because he was completely full of it. "You mean to tell me that you weren't just thinking about how I said you're a big boy?" I ran my gaze down his body and stopped directly over his groin to prove my point.

"Well, I wasn't." He ran his hand over the front of his jeans, and my gaze snapped up to meet his again. "But when you look at me like that it's all I can think about."

"What were you thinking?"

"I was thinking" —he lifted his hand and ran his thumb over my chin as he stared at my mouth— "that you have got to be the most gorgeous thing I have ever laid eyes on."

Even though I knew I shouldn't allow it, my heart sped up at his words. Carson was good at this, and I didn't stand a chance around him. It was the reason I needed to give us space. Just like at the pool, being around him did nothing but mess with my head and made me forget all the things he had done and things he had said. I would be an idiot to forget any of that.

It didn't matter what was going on at home. What I now knew he was dealing with. None of those things were an excuse for Carson to be an asshole.

And that was exactly what he had been over and over again, and I didn't know if I could trust him. After everything we had been through, I didn't know if I could trust Carson not to hurt me again.

"I was also thinking about how grateful I am that you brought my mom home." I saw a flash of shame in his eyes, and I hated it. I desperately wanted to take that away from him. "You didn't have to do that."

"I did." I nodded my head because even if he was the last person on earth I should want to protect, everything inside of me still desperately wanted to. "I didn't want her to drive home."

He hesitated for a second; I didn't know what he was going to say. I didn't know if he was going to try to hide the fact that she had been drinking or convince me that I didn't see what I thought I saw. But the next words that left his mouth shocked me. "I'm sorry you had to see that. She's been drinking a lot lately."

A nugget of truth from him. From the real Carson.

"I didn't realize that." I shook my head because I felt like I owed him something. Some explanation or some apology of why I hadn't been there for him, but we both knew that I didn't. He was the one who pushed me away, who had forced me out of his life, but maybe I should've tried harder. I didn't realize what he was going through at home. I knew that his father had cheated, and from what I've heard through the chatter at the country club, he still did.

But I never really stopped to think about how badly it had been affecting him.

"I'm sorry."

He shook his head, and I knew that he hated my apology before the words even left my mouth. "You have nothing to be sorry for."

"It's just that if I had known, I would've... I don't know. I would've done something."

"There's nothing you could have done, Allie." He chuckled, but there wasn't a trace of humor in his laugh. "My parents are beyond fucked up. There's nothing anyone can do at this point."

"That's not true." I reached out and gripped his fingers in mine, and his gaze immediately snapped to my touch.

"It is." He turned his hand over and toyed with my fingers in his. "You don't think I've tried everything to help my mom at this point? She's going to do what she wants to do."

"And your dad?" I knew this was probably the last thing he wanted to talk about, but I was desperate to know more about him. Once upon a time, I had known him better than anyone, but now I felt like a stranger.

"My dad is the same piece of shit that he's always been. He cares as little about her as he does about me."

I closed my eyes because I didn't want to believe what he was saying. Even if it was true, I couldn't imagine Carson here with a parent who didn't care about him and another who was too intoxicated to even notice. His mom had been so nice and such a good mother at one point, and it felt unbelievable that this is who she had become. "I'm sorry, Carson. I wish I had known. I wish you weren't dealing with all of this alone."

"Stop apologizing to me."

I watched him intently, and I knew that he was about to push me away. I was getting too close to something real, to something that wasn't covered by his cocky smile and a few quick jokes, and I knew that he would push and push until I was no longer anywhere near it.

"Are you heading home?" He looked toward the door and my stomach dropped.

"Is that what you want?"

"I'm not exactly sure how you want me to answer that." He was staring at my mouth, and the urge to lean forward on my tippy toes and kiss him was overwhelming. "Yesterday, you would barely speak to me, but today, what? You want to stay over and sleep together like old times?"

"I had no intention of talking to you today either." I could feel him sharpening his dagger, waiting to say something that would plunge it straight into my heart. I knew this was his way of protecting himself. "If it wasn't for your mother, I wouldn't have talked to you at all."

He stepped even closer to me and closed any space that was left between us. "So what? Were you there to cheer on Eli or is there somebody else you have your eye on now?"

"Why would it matter to you anyway?"

He brought his hand up and gripped my jaw in his hand.

His touch was almost painful, but I didn't budge. I let him have whatever he needed as I stared up at him with as much strength as I possibly possessed. "You know that it fucking matters."

"You say that. But then you do this. You want me to leave. You want to push me away because, what? I saw something real for the first time?" I tried to catch my breath as he leaned forward and rubbed his nose along my jawline.

His touch was the gentlest of caresses and was in complete contrast with the roughness of his fingers. This was Carson's specialty. Screwing me up so badly in the head that I didn't know up from down. I couldn't remember why I hated him or why I shouldn't want him. The only thing that mattered, the only thing I could feel, was him, and he knew it.

"I don't want you to leave." I barely heard his words. They were the softest whisper, and I wasn't even sure if they were intended for me to hear. But they also screamed so loudly that my body vibrated with the meaning. He would never admit to it, but he wanted me to stay because he needed me in a way that made him uncomfortable.

I hated that I needed him just as badly.

"You're right. Maybe this is a bad idea." I tried to pull away from his touch, but he didn't allow it. He just held me against him as he breathed in and out, his breath rushing against my skin, and I felt that rush of breath over every inch of me.

"I'm not." He shook his head against me. "I'm so fucking stupid when it comes to you."

I turned my head to get a better look at him but that did nothing but bring our mouths closer together. "What do you want from me, Carson?"

He hesitated before he answered, and for a moment, I thought he might not answer at all. But then he said one word that clouded any and every decision I would ever make. "Stay."

I nodded my head against him instantly, and his hand on my jaw tightened before moving around my back. He pulled me against him, impossibly close, before he gripped my thighs in his hands and lifted them around his waist.

"Your mom," I hissed, because there was no way in hell I was going to let her see me in such a compromising position with her son. Even if she had been drinking, there was no mistaking the way he was holding me or what we were planning to do.

He pressed his lips against my neck and took a deep breath, inhaling me. "She won't come out of her room for the rest of the night."

"I don't care." His hips settled against mine and my body shook beneath him. "Take me to your room."

CHAPTER 10
CARSON

I should have let her leave.

She shouldn't have been here in the first place, but now that she was, I couldn't let her walk away. Not tonight. Not when I felt so damn edgy from seeing my mom at the game or by seeing Allie taking care of her.

I climbed up the stairs with her in my arms, and she giggled when I almost tripped over the last step.

"Don't drop me." Her arms tightened around my shoulders.

"Do you really think I would drop you?" I cupped her ass in my hands as I backed her up toward my bedroom door.

"I do." She nodded and that playful smile was still on her face. "You're known for letting me down."

My steps faltered at her words, and even though they were the truth, they sliced through me.

"Shit. I'm sorry." She tried to get out of my hold, but I refused to allow her. "I shouldn't have said that."

"No." I shook my head. "It's okay. You're right."

I opened my bedroom door and pushed inside. I didn't

stop until I laid her back on my unmade bed and stood over her. She was looking up at me, and she looked like a fucking dream. A dream that I had been hellbent on ruining.

"I have let you down so many times, and I don't want to let you down ever again." She turned her head as if she was trying to block out my words, but I leaned forward, pressing my knee into the mattress between her thighs, and lifted my fingers to her chin. I turned her head back to look at me, and my heart pounded in my chest. "Let me prove it to you."

I ran my hand up her thigh and lifted it until it settled against my side. "Let me show you just how fucking good I can be to you."

When she didn't immediately say no, I took the chance and leaned forward enough to press my lips to hers. She didn't hold back. She kissed me like she was drowning and I was her savior.

She kissed me like she was trying to believe this fucked-up fairy tale where the two of us could be something regardless of our past. I wanted to make her believe it too. I wanted to take away every bit of doubt that I had planted in her and fucking erase it. I was desperate to take back all of the things I had done and said.

But I knew that I couldn't do that. I would never be able to erase our past. All I could do was make her believe in me from this moment forward.

I pushed my fingers into her hair and ran my tongue over her bottom lip. She chased my tongue with her mouth, and her hands roamed over my body in a rush. I knew exactly what she wanted, what she was after, but I refused to give her a quick fuck that gave her pleasure long enough until she remembered why she hated me.

I was going to take my time with her. Something I had never truly done with anyone else.

I kissed down her jaw and down her neck until my lips were pressed against her speeding pulse. I pushed my tongue against it and reminded myself that she was here. She was beneath me, in my hands, and this was real.

"Carson," she whimpered my name and the sound went directly to my cock.

I lapped at her skin and continued to work my way down. I nipped at her collarbone before tracing that same spot with my tongue. She writhed beneath me, and God, she felt so good.

I lifted her t-shirt in my hand, bunching it up to expose her soft stomach, and I lowered myself enough to trace my lips and tongue and teeth over every bit of exposed skin I could find.

Allie tugged on my hair, her touch almost painful, as she tried to force me exactly where she wanted me. I didn't give her that control. Instead, I lifted her shirt even higher, so slowly, as I watched her breasts rise and fall with each and every inhale. I pulled it over her head and dropped it on the ground behind me.

She was wearing the simplest light purple bra that was so thin I could see her nipples beneath before I leaned forward and brought one into my mouth over the fabric.

"Oh my God." She pulled harder against me as she began grinding her pussy against me.

I tugged the cup covering the other breast down roughly before cupping her supple skin in my hand. She felt so fucking good, too good, and I knew that I was beyond lucky that she had chosen to give me this.

I wasn't fucking worthy of her, especially not to be her

first, but there was no other thought in this world that turned me on more.

I was the only man who ever had his hands on her in this way. The only one who had tasted her body, who had fucked her, and I didn't want to give anyone else a chance.

She was mine whether she wanted to be or not, and I couldn't fathom anyone else having what was mine.

I pushed away from her and quickly undid the button on her shorts. I jerked them down her hips before lifting her legs in front of me and pulling them and her panties off of her completely.

She tried to drop them back to my sides, but I held her in place as I dropped to my knees in front of her. I ran my tongue over the back of one of her perfect fucking thighs, and she jumped. Chill bumps pebbled along her skin, and I traced them. A lap of my tongue here, a nip of my teeth there.

I continued to do so, my hand holding just above her knees to keep her legs in place, and I worked my way up to her pussy before skipping over it to taste the other side.

"I swear to God, Carson," she growled my name, and it was almost enough to dive into her and give her exactly what she wanted.

"What, baby?" I ran my tongue along the side of her pussy, careful not to touch. "Tell me exactly what you want."

"You know what I want." She squirmed beneath me, but it wasn't enough.

"Tell me," I growled and nipped at her thigh. She moaned long and loud, and it was like the sweetest fucking kryptonite. "I need to hear you tell me exactly what you want from me. Take your time." I ran my tongue over the small crease where her ass met her pussy. "I need to know that you're not going to regret this tomorrow."

She huffed in frustration before she spoke again. "I want you to..." She hesitated as her voice trembled, and I pressed the softest kiss to her skin. "I want you to taste me. I want you to put your mouth everywhere, then I want you inside me."

I barely let her finish her sentence before I was on her. I pressed my tongue to the base of her pussy, and I rolled it all the way up until it ran over her clit. She moaned, and I didn't stop. I held her legs in place as I dove into her. I held nothing back. I ate her like I was fucking starved, and I was.

I was starved for anything and everything she would give me.

She was dripping wet, and I fucking loved it. I let her legs fall to the sides, and I pressed a hand into each thigh to spread them as far apart as they could go. I didn't give her a single moment to get used to the change. I sucked her clit into my mouth, causing her back to bow off the bed and her gaze to slam into mine.

There was no need for me to tell her to watch me. She was doing that all on her own. Her eyes didn't leave mine as I pushed a finger inside her or as I added a second. It wasn't until I curled them inside of her while sucking her into my mouth that her eyes rolled back, and she slammed her hands against her mouth to quiet her cries.

Her pussy clenched around my fingers over and over, milking her pleas from me, but I didn't stop until her thighs clenched around my head and her back was completely lifted off the bed in pleasure. She came against my tongue before she sank back down to the bed, and I pulled my fingers out of her only to move them to her hips.

I flipped her over onto her stomach before I stood, then I brought her up onto her knees. Her legs were trembling beneath my hands, her orgasm still rushing through her, and I held her firmly against me while tugging my jeans down my hips.

She looked back at me as I ran my cock up and down her pussy, coating myself in her wetness, and she felt like the sweetest torture.

I pushed inside her with a loud groan that I couldn't hold back. I stared down at her as I moved inside her body, and it felt like a fucking dream. Her body was so goddamn perfect, the way she moved against me did nothing but increase my hunger, and the sound of her whimper was my kryptonite.

I pounded into her over and over, the sound of our fucking echoing around my room, and I knew I was going to come before I even got the chance to thoroughly enjoy her body. I wanted to tease her, to have her begging for me, but I wasn't capable of withholding anything from her. Not when I was so desperate for anything she was willing to give me.

I leaned forward, kissing along her spine before I pressed my hand against her chest and lifted her to me. I pushed back on my heels, my weight resting on my knees, and she molded to my body as I continued to push inside her.

My fingers found her clit, and I matched the speed of my cock as I rubbed that sensitive bundle of nerves. She palmed her own breasts, and I stared down at the rough way her fingers dug into her skin.

I kissed her neck before gripping her chin in my hand and turning her face to meet mine. I sealed my mouth over hers, desperate to taste her, and I trailed my other hand down her body until my fingers were covering hers.

I moved my hand at the same speed as her, the same

roughness, and she moaned in my mouth. Our kiss was as frantic as our bodies, a clash of lips, tongues, and teeth. We were chasing the rush that I had never felt with anyone other than her.

It was a rush and an overwhelming feeling, and I couldn't stop it even if I wanted to. This girl was everything I could want and everything I didn't deserve.

"Carson," she whimpered my name as she tightened around me, and I didn't stand a chance. I came with a loud groan, and she cried out as her body shook against mine.

I dropped to the bed, pulling her down with me, and both of us tried to calm our breathing as I held her to my chest. We didn't bother cleaning up or moving a single inch away from each other. I simply pulled the blanket over us, and I was lulled into sleep with her warm body against mine.

CHAPTER 11

ALLIE

I let the girls talk me into going to another baseball game even though I knew I shouldn't. Apparently, there were only a few games left, and the games they were now playing would determine whether or not they would go to the championship.

A championship they had been in every year since they were freshmen.

Carson was back to playing, and I knew that he knew I was here. His gaze would search me out every so often and clash with mine. I didn't know how he was even paying attention to what was happening by how often he was looking at me, but somehow he did. He played just as well as he always did, and I knew that any college team in the country would have been idiots not to pick him up.

We had barely spoken since the other night at his house, but that was only a couple days ago. We had gone way longer between talking before, but for some reason, this time it put me on edge.

He had called me last night, but I didn't answer. I didn't

know what to say to him or how to act or how to keep my head on straight whenever he was involved. I knew that whatever he asked of me I would give him, but I couldn't just give in to him because that was what he wanted.

I had no idea where his head was at, of what he truly wanted from me, and there was no way I was going to give him any more of myself while he held himself back.

But I was going to have to face him tonight. The game was almost over, and Clermont Prep was winning by a land-slide. Josie and Frankie already told me that we were plan-ning to go out to eat after to celebrate, and I would look like a pansy if I just bounced.

I didn't need him to know that I was completely avoiding him.

But I couldn't think about food or eating or anything other than him. My mind was filled with thoughts of him and the way he touched me. The way he had held me the other night like I was the most important thing to him in the world was burned into my memory, and I couldn't stop myself from reading too much into it. I was dissecting every touch, analyzing every look.

Those thoughts ran over and over through my mind. Thoughts of him, of his mom, his dad, of what he was going through. If my mind wasn't already clouded with Carson, it definitely was now.

"I'm going to head to the bathroom," I said to Frankie, but she was so engrossed in the end of the game I wasn't even sure she heard me.

I walked past the concession stand and waited in line for the bathroom. Part of me considered texting the girls and telling them that I would see them tomorrow. But I refused to be such a chicken. I would have to face him sooner or later whether I wanted to or not, and the longer I put it off, the worse it was going to be.

After everything we had done together the other night, I shouldn't have been concerned or embarrassed to be around him in any way. I let him do things to me that I hadn't even imagined possible, and I had thought about it every night since then while my hand sank into my panties and I called out his name.

He was still the only thing I was thinking about when I came out of the bathroom and almost ran straight into someone walking by.

"Oh! I'm sorry." I rushed to apologize before I looked up and saw Eli standing there in front of me. He was dressed in the same uniform as Carson, but he didn't look nearly as handsome. Part of me knew that was simply because of how I felt about him now. After I finally knew the truth, but I also knew that I should have felt the same way about Carson if I was being fair.

They both took part in that bet, even if Carson said he was only doing so to protect me.

"Hey, Allie." He grinned down at me as he adjusted his baseball bag on his shoulder, and once upon a time, I would have been so charmed by that smile on his face. But now it made my stomach turn. "You here to watch Carson play?"

I wanted to lie to him and tell him that I wasn't or that it was none of his business, but part of me just wanted to push the knife in a little deeper. I wanted to let him know that even though he had made his stupid bet about me, that yes I was here to see Carson. I wanted to rub his face in it and make him regret anything he had ever done.

So instead of doing what was smart, I nodded my head

before I spoke. "Yes. I'm here with the girls to cheer him on. Is the game over?"

The smile dropped from his face, and I knew that that wasn't what he expected me to say. That fake smile was gone, not a trace of it left on his face as anger took over.

"It is. You really have a thing for punishment, huh?" he sneered and ran his hand through his sweaty hair. "Carson Hale cares as little about you now as he did when he entered the bet. God, if you could hear the stories he told us about you."

I straightened my spine and tried to take a calming breath. I knew that Eli was probably lying, but Carson had been so cold to me then. He was cruel and bitter and angry, and it was not out of the realm of possibility that what he was saying was true.

I shrugged my shoulders and tried to pretend like I didn't care but he could see straight through me. "What Carson did in the past doesn't really interest me."

I started to walk away when his voice stopped me in my tracks. Eli wasn't done with me, trying to break me for whatever reason.

"It should interest you." He chuckled without humor. "According to him, you gave him your virginity the night you were supposed to be in the tent with me. Do you know how many people he's been with, Allie? How many girls he's fucked and left? You did nothing but become exactly what he wanted you to do. He made you another one of his whores who he doesn't have to do anything for other than get you off."

I stared at him, and everything inside of me begged me to step forward and slap him across his smug face. But I wouldn't give him that satisfaction. I wouldn't allow him to know how badly his words affected me. "If that was what you wanted, you should've just told me. I wouldn't have wasted my time trying to date you if I knew all you needed was a good fuck."

"Don't say that to me." I took a step away from him.

"Why not?" He grinned before taking a step closer to me. "That's what Carson says about you. He brags to the entire team about how willing you are and how desperate you have become for his touch. I know that he's all you've ever had, but I guarantee that I could make it better. I could make you come harder than Carson could ever dream."

He stepped closer still, and I stumbled back to get away from him. This was a side of Eli I had never seen before. Even through the bet and finding out the truth, he had never acted like this, and I hated seeing it now.

"Carson is right over there." I pointed behind me toward the field, and I didn't know why I said it.

"Do you really think I care? What exactly do you think he's going to do? Come over here and save his little whore?" he sneered at me before taking the time to run his gaze over my entire body. I felt so violated by that single look.

"He kicked your ass at baseball practice, didn't he?" My hand shook as I pulled my phone out of my back pocket. I had two missed calls from Frankie, and I knew that they'd come looking for me if I didn't return soon.

My finger hovered over Frankie's name as I watched Eli. I didn't think he would really hurt me. I didn't think he was capable of it. Not physically, at least. Eli liked to run his mouth, he had proven that time and again.

"He didn't do shit," he spit out at me, and I knew that was the wrong thing to say. "He's nothing but a spoiled asshole who only wants you because I did. Did he tell you that he turned down the bet at first?" He stepped even closer, and I held my breath. "He wasn't interested until he found out that I was going to fuck you. How fucking insane do you think he would go if I fucked you now?"

"That will never happen." My voice shook but my words were firm.

"It could." He nodded his head. "Tell me what it'll take, and I'll do it. Tell me what it is you like."

I looked down at my phone and found Carson's name before I could think better of it. I brought it to my ear as it rang, and Eli watched me like a hawk.

"Hey, Allie." His voice was smooth and gentle, and for some reason, it made a ball form in my throat.

"I need you to come get me." It was the only thing I could think to say. The only thing that I knew.

"Where are you?" His answer was instant and sounded nothing like it did just a moment before.

"Outside the bathroom."

Eli chuckled and stepped back with his hands raised in the air. I didn't drop the phone from my ear, and I could hear Carson breathing on the other end as he came for me.

"Don't say I didn't warn you." Eli looked to the side before taking off in that direction. "Carson Hale is nothing but a fuckboy, sweetheart."

He disappeared into the darkening parking lot, and I sagged against the wall. I didn't know what I was expecting him to do or why my heart hammered in my chest, but I knew that I didn't trust Eli. Not one single bit.

Carson was saying something through the phone, but I couldn't hear him over my moment of panic.

Eli was more than angry about what happened between me and Carson and about what didn't happen between me and him, but he had no right. He was the one who made that stupid bet. He had no real interest in me. His only concern was that Carson took something from him that he had wanted.

That he thought belonged to him.

But I didn't belong to anyone. Especially not him.

I was still thinking about everything he said when Carson rounded the corner in a rush and his panicked eyes met mine. He was still holding his phone to his ear, but when his gaze met mine, he pushed it into his pocket.

He was on me within a second, his hands roaming over my face, and his eyes searching mine. "What's wrong?"

I shook my head and looked past him to search the parking lot. "I... he..."

"Who?" His voice no longer had a trace of calmness. "What the fuck happened, baby?"

"I was coming out of the bathroom, and I ran into Eli."

Carson's body stiffened in front of me, his hands like statues against my skin.

"He was just talking shit and saying things that I know aren't true, but I don't know." I shook my head. "He didn't do anything, but I was starting to feel uncomfortable."

I searched his face before I said the next words. "He got so close to me, and he said things that just made me freak out for a moment. I'm sorry I called you."

"What?" he growled. "Do not apologize to me for shit you have no business apologizing for." He stepped away from me, and I knew that he was going to go find Eli. I knew it more than I knew anything else, and I knew that whatever happened between them wouldn't be pretty.

"Carson." I gripped his jersey in my hand and held on to him like I never intended to let go. "Please don't leave me."

He looked so torn as he looked from me back out to the parking lot. "I will kill him, Allie." His words lanced through me like an oath.

"He's not worth it." I pulled him closer to me and wrapped my hands around his neck to force him to look at me. "He's just angry and talking out of that anger."

"He may not be, but you are." I tried to not let his words sear me, but it was too late. It didn't matter if he was speaking out of anger or protectiveness. I couldn't stop myself from taking them in and making my heart beat to the sound of them. "I will wreck the whole damn world to protect you."

He pressed his lips to my forehead, and they trembled against my skin. "What did he say to you?"

It was at that moment that our friends rounded the corner, and I could see the slight panic on both Josie's and Frankie's faces.

"Are you okay?" Frankie came up beside me, and if she could feel the anger rolling off of Carson, she didn't show it. She pulled me toward her, but I clasped my hand in Carson's and held on to it as I hugged her. "What happened?"

"Nothing." I shook my head.

"Bullshit," Carson cursed and his hand tightened in mine.

He looked at Beck and Olly, and he was conveying a message to them that I wasn't sure I wanted to know.

"Eli is fucking lucky he wasn't still here when I got to you."

"Eli was here?" Josie's gaze snapped to mine, and I knew that she wanted me to explain everything that had happened. I wasn't sure if I could. I felt too emotional. Too raw.

"Yeah." I nodded and looked back at Carson. "He was just saying a bunch of stupid crap."

"Like what?" The way Carson asked the question told me that he wasn't playing around. He wanted to know what Eli said to me even if I didn't want to tell him.

"He was telling me about how Carson had made me another one of his..." I hesitated because I didn't want to say it.

"My what?" Carson demanded.

"He said that I had become one of your whores and that you told the whole team about it." His hand stiffened in mine, and I tried to blow it off like it wasn't that big of a deal. "It doesn't matter what he said."

"It does." Carson swallowed and pulled me against his chest. My chest hit his, and I stared up at him. "You know that isn't fucking true."

"It doesn't matter." I shook my head before he gripped my jaw in his trembling hand and forced me to look back at him. I was acutely aware of our friends standing next to us, and they could hear every word we said. Carson didn't seem to care one bit.

"You are not a whore, and I haven't said shit to anyone about what has happened between us." I knew what he meant, but that messed up part of my brain went straight to the thought that maybe he didn't want anyone to know about us. He knew it too. "The only thing that they know is that I've made it perfectly fucking clear that you are off-limits to all of them. You may not want to be with me, but I refuse to allow you to be with any of them. They don't deserve you."

"I didn't..." I shook my head again because I didn't know what he wanted me to say. It wasn't that I didn't want to be with him. I desperately did, but I didn't know if I could trust him. After everything that had happened between us, I didn't know if I could ever truly put myself in the position that handed my heart to him for him to do with as he pleased.

Giving him my body was one thing, but everything beyond that was different. Even though, deep down, I knew he already had it. Carson has had my heart since we were kids, and I wasn't sure that I would ever be able to get it back. Not really.

"We don't have to talk about this now." His thumb pushed into my chin, and I looked back up at him. "Come home with me."

"I don't think that's a good idea."

"Either you come home with me or I'm coming home with you." He searched my eyes as he held on to me. "But there's no way I'm going to be away from you tonight."

My stomach tightened even harder, and there was a rush of feelings and emotions that were coursing through me. I didn't know how to explain and understand a single one of them.

"My dad will shit himself if I try to sneak you into my bedroom."

His smirk felt like a breath of fresh air after facing his anger. "Then tell your mom you're staying with Josie and come home with me."

"I could just go home with Josie and Frankie. Beck will be there."

He pulled me closer to him with his hand on my chin and didn't stop until his forehead pressed against mine. "That's not fucking happening, baby." He pressed his lips so gently against mine that I was worried I was imagining them. "Okay?"

"Okay." I nodded, and he finally let me go.

"Are you sure you're okay?" Josie looked between me and Carson, and I knew what she was really asking. She wanted to know if I really wanted to go home with him. Because if I didn't, she wouldn't care how pissed off he was.

"I am now." I nodded and wrapped her in a hug. It was only a second later when I felt Frankie wrap herself around my back.

Once they let go of me, Carson took my hand in his and led me to his car.

"I drove." I pointed down the parking lot, but he shook his head.

"That's not happening. I need you with me."

I didn't argue. I let him open my door, and I climbed inside. He moved around the car quickly, and we were driving away by the time I had my seatbelt buckled.

Carson was so quiet. Too damn quiet.

"Carson, I..."

"You know what he said isn't true, right?" His hands tightened around the steering wheel. "You are not what he says, and I wouldn't dare insult you in such a way."

"I know that." I nodded, but there was so much that was still nagging at me. "But part of me wonders if he was right."

"What?" he growled.

"Not all of it, but he said that you didn't want me until you realized that he did. That you just didn't want anyone else to touch something that was yours, and I can't help thinking he was right."

The car jerked to the side as he pulled off the road, and I grabbed on to the handle. "What are you doing?"

Carson climbed out of the car without saying a word, and I watched as he paced back and forth in front of the car. I held perfectly still as he ran his fingers through his hair, tugging on the ends, and I watched as his chest rose and fell with an increasing pace.

When he didn't return after a couple of minutes, I slowly climbed out of the car and shut the door behind me. We were in an empty parking lot at the front of the school. We had barely made it a minute away from the field, but it was so dark here in comparison. It felt like we had left everyone else far behind us.

"Carson," I called out his name as I rounded the car, but he didn't stop. "Carson, please."

He finally looked at me then, and he charged toward me until my ass hit the hood of his car.

"I don't want you because Eli fucking wanted you. I want you because you're fucking spectacular. I want you because I've wanted you for as long as I can remember." He clenched and unclenched his hand before running it through his hair. "Trust me, if I could, I would give you up so you could fall for someone good."

"You are good." I raised my hand to touch his face, and he turned into my touch. He pressed a kiss to the palm of my hand.

"No. I'm not, but I'm too damn selfish to give you up." He kissed me then, pressing me further back onto his car, and I didn't hesitate as I wrapped my arms around him.

I clung to him as he kissed me, and I pushed my hips into his.

I was desperate for his touch, for him to make me forget everything that had happened with Eli.

He pulled away, just far enough for him to be able to

look at me, before he said, "I don't know what I need to do to make it up to you, for you to forgive me for what I've done, but I will. I'll do whatever it takes."

My chest warmed at his faintly uttered words, the vulnerability in them enough to make me forget everything that had ever come before this moment.

But to do so would be foolish for both of us. I could have told him that I would forgive him in that moment, that I wouldn't give a second thought to our past, but I knew that wasn't real. Even if I did forgive Carson, and part of me knew that I already had, I still felt the need to guard my heart from him.

Because that was what he had been doing for years. Guarding himself and pushing me away.

I didn't answer the vow he had just made me. Instead, I wrapped my arms around his neck and pulled him closer to me until he had no choice but to press his lips against mine.

His tongue pushed into my mouth, somehow lazy and thorough while still feeling frantic. His hands touched me everywhere. They cupped my face before moving down my neck, to my chest and then my hips.

I groaned into his mouth as I tugged on his hair, and I pushed my hips wildly against his.

"Allie," he groaned my name, the deep timbre of his voice like a drug. "We need to stop." He was still kissing me as he spoke, and his words felt meaningless. "We can't do this here."

"We can." I nodded and ground against him harder. "I need you."

"Fuck." He pushed off me far enough to undo his baseball pants, and I made quick work of pulling my skirt up to my hips. He watched me with eager eyes as I slid my panties down my legs and leaned back against his car once more.

He gripped my thighs in his hands and tugged me further down the hood until my pussy pressed against him, and he slid his thumb through my wetness that was already coating my inner thighs.

"Allie, I…"

I leaned forward and kissed him because I didn't think I could handle whatever he was going to say next. Not tonight. Not when I was already feeling vulnerable and so damn confused.

I kissed him until he completely forgot about what he planned to say, and I moaned into his mouth when he slowly slid inside me. Once he was settled to the hilt, something inside of him snapped.

His gentle touches became so rushed and rough. The way he slammed inside me at a savage pace that had me crying out his name.

He watched me with feral eyes, his need to claim me, brutal and raging, and that same need thrummed inside of me. I wanted him to mark me in a way that no one would question how he felt about me. I desperately needed him to erase the thoughts of doubts that Eli had planted in my head and replace them with his searing greed for me.

I wasn't prepared when he pulled away from me and flipped me onto my stomach or when my face pressed into the hood as he slammed back inside of me. His fingers dug into my hips as he held me in place, and I was completely at his mercy.

It didn't take long before I completely fell over the edge into my climax, and he didn't stop. He pounded into me as I came around him, and when I whimpered his name, he pulled out of me with a jerk. He held his cock against my ass as he came, his cum exploding over my skin.

He leaned against me, his forehead resting against my back, as both of us tried to catch our breaths, but it was useless. Being with him, being around him, I constantly felt like I was breathless and dazed.

I stayed that way while he cleaned me up and helped me stand before straightening my skirt, and I fell asleep with the same damn feeling after we walked hand in hand through his house and climbed into his bed.

I rested my head on his chest, and he curled his arm around me as if he needed to remind himself that I was really there. And as I drifted off to sleep, I heard him murmuring something near my head even though I couldn't make out what it was.

CHAPTER 12
CARSON

I couldn't stop thinking about Allie or the way I woke up without her there.

I had text her immediately when I found my bed cold, and she had simply sent back: **I needed to study for a test I have today. Talk later.**

Bullshit. That's exactly what her excuse was. Complete and utter bullshit. I scared her last night. I had done too much, said too much, and I didn't even know if she heard me when I had confessed things to her over her sleeping head.

I had pressed my lips to her forehead and promised to protect her. I had told her everything except the thing that truly mattered. The urge to tell her that I loved her was overwhelming, but I knew she wasn't ready to hear it.

Not when she had already experienced so much yesterday. So I let her run. I let her hide from what she was feeling for me and I didn't push her.

But now I couldn't stand it anymore. I needed to see her, to touch her, and to prove to myself that everything that happened between us last night wasn't in my imagination.

It was the reason I was parked outside of her school even though my own school day wasn't finished. I had walked out without saying a word to anyone. I knew that Coach would blow a gasket when he realized I wasn't at practice, but I couldn't bring myself to care. Things that once mattered so much seemed so insignificant compared to her.

I was parked right next to her car near the front of the school, and I sat on the hood of my car as I waited for her. Students were starting to push through the door, and I didn't miss the way most of them watched me as they walked by. I was still in my Clermont Prep uniform although I had tossed my jacket in the back seat and rolled up the sleeves of my white shirt.

I didn't pay any attention to them as they passed me. I just searched the door for her. When she finally walked out, she was carrying a few textbooks in her arms, and she was laughing with a girl who walked beside her. A girl who I had never seen before, and I realized that I barely knew this side of Allie.

The person she was when she wasn't around me and my friends.

She didn't notice me at first. She was talking animatedly and laughing, and she looked so beautiful, so carefree.

It was thrilling to watch her that way, to watch her look so happy.

She was only about a dozen feet away from me when the girl nudged her elbow into Allie's and nodded in my direction. Allie looked up at me, and she blinked as if she wasn't sure what she was seeing. Her smile dropped for a second before a completely different one formed on her beautiful face.

I didn't move a muscle. I just leaned forward, pressing

my elbows into my knees, and watched her as she walked toward me.

"Are you lost?" She stopped right in front of me, so close I could almost touch her.

"I don't think so." I shook my head. "Do I look lost to you?"

"I guess that depends." She cocked her head, and I could feel myself falling head over heels for this girl as she grinned at me.

"On what?"

"What are you here for?"

I slid down my hood and reached out and gripped her t-shirt between my fingers. I tugged her toward me until her knees bumped into mine. "You."

"And what exactly do you want with me?" She hugged her books against her chest and looked down at me. There were a million ways that I could answer her, but I don't think any of them were what she was looking for.

"Right now?" I rubbed my hand up and down her hip. "I want you to go to the boardwalk with me and then maybe dinner."

"Like a date?" she squeaked out, and it was so damn adorable.

"After the things I did to your body last night, you're embarrassed by me asking you out on a date?"

She looked around her, but no one was close enough to hear a word that I said. "I'm not embarrassed."

"You look it."

"I'm just shocked, is all. Plus, we have community service." She shrugged, and I stood, closing the space between us and grabbing the books out of her arms.

I leaned forward and pressed the softest kiss to her

cheek. "Crazier things have happened, and Mr. Sneed called and said that we were finished." I chuckled as I lied. She was finished, but I still had to go back and finish a few projects he needed my help with. But I had convinced him that she needed to focus on school because she did. "Don't make me beg."

She turned her face to look at me, and her mouth was so damn close to mine. "Would you?" She searched my eyes, and I couldn't stand it. I leaned forward and captured her mouth in a kiss. I didn't give a shit who was watching us.

"I'd get on my fucking knees." I ran my nose along her jaw before pressing a kiss just below her ear. "I'd do whatever it took for you to say yes."

She let out the tiniest moan, and it made me so fucking hard. This wasn't in my plans. I didn't come here with the intentions of getting the girl into my car and fucking her within an inch of her life. But God, that was all I could think about now.

"What do you say?"

"Okay." She nodded and took a small step back. "Let me put my stuff in my car." She took her books back from my arms before putting them and her backpack in the front seat. She straightened out her clothes as she stood and turned back to me. "I wish you had warned me. I would have worn something different."

She was wearing a pair of weathered jeans and a faded t-shirt that looked like it may have belonged to one of her parents once upon a time. "You look beautiful."

"Thank you." She smiled and ran her hands down her jeans.

"Let's go." I took her hand in mine and pulled her toward

the passenger side of my car and opened the door for her. She smiled as if she was trying to hold back a laugh. "What?"

"Nothing." She chuckled and climbed into my car.

I closed the door behind her and hurried to the other side of my car. I climbed inside and started the ignition before turning my head against the headrest to look at her.

"What?" She was still grinning, and God, that look belonged on her face.

"Just happy that you said yes." I put the car in reverse, and we barely spoke another word as I drove us to the boardwalk that was only a few minutes away. The air in the car felt so stifling, and I wondered if she was obsessing over every little move I made just like I was with her.

We climbed out of the car, and I reached out for her hand. She stared at mine for a second before she accepted it.

"This is weird," she shocked me by saying as we started walking down the boardwalk.

"What?" I looked over at her. "You don't ever come here."

"That's not what I'm talking about, and you know it."

"Then what?" I turned so I was walking backward but kept her hand in mine. "What's weird about this?"

"For one, you." She made a face that made me laugh. "You have never been this nice to me."

"That's not true." My chest ached because I knew she was right. "I used to be nice to you all the time."

"Yeah." She nodded in agreement, but that was a long time ago. "But you're different now."

"I am, but so are you."

"How so?" She blinked up at me.

"Well, you are a lot bolder than that girl I remember. A little more stubborn too." I grinned when she wrinkled her nose. "That's not a bad thing. I like that you have a back-bone, that you don't just let me get away with my shit."

"That could be argued," she huffed. "I think a lot of people think I'm pretty weak for still giving you a single moment of my time after everything you've done."

"And what do you think?" My heart pounded so hard that I thought she could hear it. I stopped us and leaned against the railing that separated the boardwalk from the beach.

"Honestly?"

"Of course." I didn't want anything if it wasn't her honesty.

"I don't know what I think. I want to say that I don't care what anyone thinks about me, but that would be a lie. I care too much, but I don't feel weak when I'm with you. I don't..." She hesitated, and I kept quiet while she tried to form her thoughts. "I don't think I've been this happy in a really long time."

I couldn't stop the smile that took over my face at her admission. I knew that took so much for her to admit, for her to put herself out there in that way.

"Me either." I tugged her toward me. "And I'm sorry that I had to be such a dick before I figured that out."

"You don't have to keep apologizing." She stared up at me, and I pushed her hair out of her face.

She was wrong. I would need to apologize to her over and over every day, and it wouldn't be enough. I wasn't sure it would ever be enough. "I do." I kissed her forehead, and she closed her eyes. She said she was happy, but I still didn't know where she stood. "I don't think I'll ever be able to make up for all I've done to you."

She didn't answer me for a long moment, and I knew that she was thinking about what I said. She was probably agreeing and considering walking away from me at that exact moment.

"Are you going to feed me?"

I laughed at her question and nodded. "Yeah." I tilted her face until she was looking directly up at me. "I can't let my girl go hungry." Then I kissed her before leading her down to the restaurant.

We were seated across from each other, and Allie couldn't stop smiling as she looked out at the ocean.

"So, what's the deal with Olly?" She took a sip of her drink.

"What do you mean?"

"Is he as in love with Frankie as I think he is or am I just a really bad judge of character?"

I laughed and leaned back in my chair. "No. I think you're spot on, but nothing can ever come of it."

"Because of Beck?" She was watching me carefully.

"Yeah." I nodded. "Once upon a time, it might have been fine, but since Lucas..." I shook my head because I hated even thinking about it. My stomach turned just thinking about the way Frankie's eyes had looked so empty for so long after everything had happened. "I don't think Beck is going to let anyone near Frankie, definitely not one of his friends."

"I understand. I do." She winced. "But he has to know that it's not up to him. Frankie looks at Olly the exact same way he looks at her. She has never admitted to it, at least not to me, but it's hard to miss."

"It is," I agreed. "I honestly don't know what will happen, but it makes me anxious."

She laughed at my admission just as our food arrived at our table.

"That's not funny."

"You're right." She held up her hands in defense. "It's not. I was just thinking about ol' playboy Carson being anxious about his friends' love lives."

"I do have a heart, you know."

"I know you do." She smiled up at me, and the urge to lean over the table and kiss her was overwhelming. So, that was exactly what I did. I stood, not giving a shit about what I knocked off the table and pressed a gentle kiss to her mouth.

Her eyes looked glazed over as I sat back down. "What was that for?"

"I just felt like it." I was honest with her.

She smiled, just the slight curve of her lips, but it was so potent that I could barely catch my breath.

She took a bite of her food before looking away from me for a moment. I was dying to know what was going on in that head of hers. I would have given anything for just the tiniest glimpse.

"I don't know what Frankie is going to do without us next year." I chuckled before taking a bite of my own food. "I bet the guys are going to come out of the woodwork once Beck has graduated."

She grinned and looked back up at me. "She'll still have me. I won't be too far."

Because she was staying here.

She would be here, and I would be, fuck, I didn't even know.

The plan had been for me, Beck, and Olly to go to the University of California for so long. It was our pact to each other, but Beck had already changed his plans. He didn't want to be too far away from his family or from Josie, and I didn't blame him. I just didn't think I'd ever be questioning my own decisions.

But the idea of leaving now felt like lead in my stomach.

"Have you decided what you're going to major in?" I tried to think about anything other than how far apart we'd be.

"I think so." She nodded. "But honestly, I don't even know what I want to eat most days. I don't know that I'm really qualified to figure out what I want to do with the rest of my life."

I laughed. "I think you're more qualified than I am. Unless baseball becomes my career, then I'm pretty much hopeless."

"You are not." She rolled her eyes and shook her head. "If baseball doesn't work out, I could see you being all sorts of things." She held up her fingers as she counted them off. "A lawyer. A sports manager. A stripper. Oh my God, you could be a teacher and coach little boys on how to play baseball."

I stared at her like she had lost her mind. "Are we just going to glaze over the fact that you just suggested I become a stripper?"

She grinned and her gaze ran down my chest. "I just meant as a last resort option." She waved her hand in my direction. "All of that is just going to waste."

"Are you objectifying me?" I pressed my hand to my chest.

"Yeah." She nodded with the biggest grin on her face. "I guess I am."

"I swear. You think you know people."

She snorted at my sarcasm. "Please be serious. I don't

need to objectify you for you to know you have all that going for you."

"Are you saying that you find me attractive?" I was teasing her, but I loved the slight blush that creeped up her neck. It fascinated me how this girl could still be embarrassed after all the things we had done to one another.

"I didn't say that. I just meant that you might have a market of women who possibly could."

"Uh-huh." I leaned closer to her and lowered my voice. "Do you normally fuck men with your mouth that you find unattractive?"

She choked on her food and her eyes searched the area around us. No one had heard me, but the look on her face was worth it.

"I did not fuck..." she hesitated on the last word, and it was so damn cute. "You with my mouth."

"You most certainly did." I adjusted my pants because I was getting hard just thinking about it. "I have never been given such good head in my life."

"Oh my God." She buried her face in her hands, and I laughed. "I cannot believe you just said that."

"It's the truth." I shrugged like we were talking about the weather. "It's the only thing I can think about when I wrap my hand..."

"Okay!" she shrieked and stood from her chair. She moved toward me, and I leaned my head back to stare up at her. "You are so..."

"Handsome, perfect, mesmerizing?" I offered her suggestions, and she shook her head.

"Lewd."

"Thank you." I reached up and wrapped my hand around the back of her neck to pull her down to me.

"I didn't mean it as a compliment." She laughed against my mouth.

"I'll take it as one anyway."

Then I kissed her and didn't hear a single other complaint about how lewd I could be.

CHAPTER 13
ALLIE

"What should we do now?" My fingers twisted around his as we walked.

"How about a tattoo?" He nodded to the shop that was just up ahead.

My heart raced at the thought. "Okay."

"What?" He looked down at me in shock. "I was just fucking around."

"Why not?" I shrugged my shoulders and pulled him toward the shop. "You don't have any, do you?"

He cocked an eyebrow. "You know I don't."

"I haven't seen every little part of your body." I rolled my eyes at the way his smile became so cocky.

"You haven't?" He tugged me toward him as we neared the entrance and wrapped his hands around my back. "So you're telling me we should probably skip the tattoo and get naked instead?"

"I did not say that." I giggled as his nose ran along the sensitive skin of my neck.

"I think that's exactly what you said." He kissed my jaw,

and it felt so weird how freely he was giving me his affection. "Something about how you needed to explore every inch of my body before we could determine what tattoo would be best."

"Carson Hale." I pulled away from him enough to get a good look at his face. "If I didn't know any better, I would say that you're scared."

"I am not scared." He shook his head and looked past me to the shop. "I'm just not a fan of making rash decisions."

I laughed because he was so full of crap. "You are the king of rash decisions."

"So, we're doing this then? No talking you out of it."

"Nope." I grinned and opened the door. "You shouldn't have asked if you didn't want to go through with it."

"I thought you were a chicken." He laid his arm over my shoulders and pulled me to him as we headed toward the counter. "That was poor judgment on my part."

"You should really stop underestimating me."

"Hi!" A middle-aged woman with bright pink hair grinned at us. "What can I do for you guys?"

"We'd like to get a tattoo." I bounced on my toes as I answered her.

"Okay." She nodded with a warm smile on her face. "I'm assuming you all don't have an appointment."

"We don't." I deflated a little and Carson grinned.

"No worries. I'm sure we can squeeze you in as long as you're not getting anything huge. Do you know what you want?"

"I do." I nodded my head, and Carson looked at me like I was crazy.

"How do you know what you want? We just decided to do this two seconds ago."

"Because I've wanted to get one for a while." I tapped my phone because I've had the image saved there for months.

"Let me see." He reached for my phone, but I tugged it out of his reach.

"No." I chuckled. "You can see it once it's done."

"What if I want to get the same tattoo?" He arched an eyebrow and toyed with my fingers in his.

"You don't." I shook my head. "It's not really your style."

"I'm guessing you'll be going first then." The receptionist looked at me, and I nodded.

"He's a bit scared so I need to show him that it's nothing to worry about."

She bit her bottom lip to stop laughing. "Okay." She clicked on her computer. "I need to get some identification from both of you, then I'll introduce you to the artist."

We did as she asked, and both Carson and I gave her our IDs. I was thrumming with excitement as I showed the artist the tattoo that I wanted. He drew the most delicate sunshine I had ever seen, the nickname my parents had called me for most of my life, before printing the words *come what may* beneath it.

"Are you really not going to show me before you get it?" Carson asked as the tattoo artist pressed the small stencil just below my inner elbow.

"No. I don't need you talking me out of it."

"Oh, God." He ran his hand over his face where he sat in the corner of the room. "Please tell me you are not getting my name tattooed on you."

"You wish."

The tattoo artist pulled off the stencil, and it looked so perfect. "What do you think?"

"It's perfect."

He finished setting up, and I held my breath as the tattoo gun first touched my skin.

"What do you think your parents are going to say?" Carson was leaning forward with his elbows on his knees as he watched me.

"Nothing they really can say. My mom has a tattoo."

"No. She doesn't." He chuckled, and I grinned.

"She does." I winced at the pain. "She has the smallest outline of a wave tattooed on her hip."

"I don't know why, but that makes me like your mom even more than I already did."

"Me too." I nodded and tried to distract myself by talking to him. "Plus, if they do get mad, I'll just blame it on you and say that you were a bad influence."

He laughed, deep and throaty, and I closed my eyes as the sound washed over me. "Your mom loves me. She would never believe that."

"She might." I peeked an eye open and looked back at him. "But my dad is a harder nut to crack."

"Are you saying he doesn't like me?"

"No. I'm just saying that he would believe his baby over the big bad Carson Hale who's known for his reputation."

Carson snorted, and I couldn't help but laugh.

"How long have the two of you been dating?" My artist smiled up at me before dipping his gun in more ink.

"Oh, we're not..." I answered at the same time Carson said, "Unofficially, about a month."

"We have not been dating a month."

"I said unofficially." He shrugged like that was the only explanation I needed.

I looked away from him and back to the guy permanently marking my skin. "We're not dating. He's just my friend."

"If you say so." He chuckled and kept tattooing.

"See. Even he knows that you should stop denying this." Carson waved back and forth between us, and if I wasn't already preoccupied, I would have smacked him.

So, instead, I just ignored him as I breathed through the pain, and he didn't say another word until we were finished. I stood from my chair and looked in the mirror. It was perfect. Absolutely perfect.

"I love it."

Carson stood, coming behind me, and he rested his chin on the top of my head as he stared at my tattoo in the mirror. "Come what may," he read the quote aloud.

I nodded my head and looked up to meet his gaze in the mirror.

"I think that's perfect for you."

For us. I felt like those words were on the tip of his tongue, but maybe they were just pounding away in my heart. Because come what may, I didn't think I would be able to walk away from Carson again. I didn't think I would be able to give him up.

He pressed a kiss to my temple before he let me go. "My turn."

"Do you know what you're getting?" I moved back to the artist and let him wrap up my brand new work.

"I do." He nodded and ran his fingers through his hair. He looked nervous, and it was the most endearing thing I had ever seen. This man, who was always so damn full of himself, looked like he could possibly pass out at any moment.

"What did you decide on?"

"I'm not telling you." He shook his head and paced in front of me.

"Really? You didn't even know what you wanted five minutes ago."

"All is fair." He winked at me, then I left the room while he and the same artist who had just done my tattoo talked over his design.

I stared down at my new artwork and smiled. I took a quick photo with my phone and sent it to Josie and Frankie in a group chat.

My phone beeped instantly with an incoming message, but I was too distracted by Carson saying, "Fuck it. Let's go," to check it.

I walked back into the room and saw the artist marking Carson in the same spot he had just done me except on the opposite arm. I sat down in the corner exactly where Carson had been, and I leaned forward to try to get a glimpse.

"No peeking," Carson chastised me, and I laughed.

"What do you think your parents are going to say?" I asked his same question from earlier. "If I had to put money on it, I'd say neither one of them has any hidden ink."

"You would be correct." He leaned his head back against the headrest and looked at me. "My dad will probably have a heart attack."

"You don't have to get it if you're going to get in trouble."

The tattoo gun suddenly stopped, but Carson quickly answered. "Oh, hell no. There's no way I'm going to let you talk shit about me for the rest of my life because you think I chickened out."

I grinned because he was so ridiculous.

"Plus, everyone already knows that you're a bad influence on me. It won't take any convincing on my part."

"No one on this planet would believe that I could possibly have any kind of influence over you."

"Oh, love, but you do." He looked at me so dreamily that I felt like I couldn't breathe. I could feel my blush heating up my face as my gaze met the tattoo artist's before snapping back to Carson's.

The way he watched me was so poignant and tender. If he was feeling any pain from the tattoo, he wasn't letting it show. But I squirmed. I was overwhelmed and so damn confused, but I couldn't look away from him even for a second.

I felt like I had walked too close to a fire, burning and mesmerized, but I couldn't stop.

"All done." The tattoo artist's words made me jump in my seat, and Carson finally looked away from me to look down at his arm.

"Thank you." His voice was gruff, and I wondered if he had just felt as entranced as I had.

The artist wrapped his tattoo in the same clear film that he had mine, but I felt like I couldn't stand. I was desperate to see what he got, to see the ink that marked his skin, but my heart was clouded, and my chest ached.

Carson stood, looking back to me as he clapped hands with the artist, and I tried to breathe.

It was no use.

He turned in my direction, his arm in clear view, and I stared at the words on his arm. Come what may.

Come what may. The words stared back at me, and I couldn't pull my gaze away long enough to look at him.

"A moon," he said, and I brought my attention to the crescent moon that rested above the words. The exact opposite of my sun. He said nothing else, but he didn't need to. I saw it there hidden in his eyes, words that neither one of us were brave enough to say, but it didn't matter.

I stood, my feet sure and my heart battering against my chest, and I kissed him, this boy who I had loved as long as the sun had loved the moon. And I didn't stop until my breath was frenzied and shredded.

I kissed him until I was sure he knew that no matter what came after this moment, I loved him. I loved him and everything he was, and there was nothing that could change that.

CHAPTER 14
CARSON

I felt like I was high.

Fuck, it felt better than any high I had ever had before. I was happy.

Allie made me deliriously happy, and even though that feeling alone scared me, it felt far too good to ever give away willingly. I had been an idiot for so damn long when it came to her, and I knew that if I wanted to keep her that it was going to take more than I had ever given before.

I owed that girl a lifetime of apologies, a lifetime of nights just like tonight where the smile wouldn't dare fall from her face.

Where she looked so damn free that it was hard to remember her as anything else. She was mesmerizing and daunting and so fucking unforgettable.

She always had been.

I couldn't think about anything but her and the way she had smiled over at me while I drove her home or the way her fingers had trailed over mine like she was trying to solve a puzzle.

Her touch still felt like a ghost against my skin as I gripped my steering wheel and turned onto my street. I was still stuck in the overwhelming feel of her when I noticed the red and blue lights flashing and ricocheting off every available surface.

My heart raced and I held my breath as I searched for the source of the light. My foot was heavy against the pedal as I raced toward my house, and my heart stopped when I realized I had found them.

I slammed my car into park directly behind the firetruck that was blocking the view of our front door, and I didn't bother pulling my keys out of the ignition before jumping out of the car. I couldn't think or feel anything as I ran toward my house.

Absently, I noticed a few police cars and an ambulance parked next to the entrance, but I ran past them all. I didn't stop until my feet hit the hard tile of our entryway where I found my dad tugging at the ends of his hair.

He looked upset, but not in his typical fashion. This was different. Something was different.

"Dad," I called his name, but I barely heard my own voice over the loud ringing in my ears.

"Carson." There was a harsh look of fear and regret that passed over his face, and panic took over as I searched the rest of the faces that crowded my house for the one I would recognize.

I searched for the one face that mattered.

But I couldn't find her.

I pushed through them, my shoulder knocking into one of the officers as I tried to get to her bedroom. His arms came down around me, and I tried to jerk away from his touch. This was my fucking house, and I needed to find her.

"Carson," my father barked out my name again, but I still wasn't listening. I knew something was wrong with her, and I should have been here. She needed me, and I wasn't going to let my father or any of these men who didn't matter for one single second stand in my way.

"Carson, stop!"

I looked over at my father, and I tried to calm down. I tried to will my heart to quit racing and for my chest to stop feeling like it was cracking open. "Where's my mother?"

No one said anything for a few long seconds that felt like hours, and the urge to scream at them was overwhelming.

"Where is she?"

My father stepped closer to me as the officer loosened his grip on me, and just looking at him tasted bitter.

"Carson."

If he said my name one more time, I was going to kill him. "What did you do?"

"There was an accident, Carson." He searched my face, but his eyes were fucking hollow just like him. He was a shell of the man that I used to look up to. He was nothing like the man who I once wanted to be. "You know your mom has been really sick."

"What the fuck are you talking about?" I stepped toward him and noticed one of the officers shift in my direction out of the corner of my eye. I didn't give a shit about him. "Where is she?" My voice echoed off the empty walls of this sad fucking house, and I watched my dad flinch.

"She's in our room..."

I immediately pushed past the officers to get to her when his voice stopped me in my tracks. "You shouldn't see her like this, Carson. She wouldn't want you to."

I kept walking but his voice followed me step for step. I

tried to block out his words, but I couldn't. Every syllable was like a slice through my chest. Every part of me tried to recoil and hide from what he was saying, but the safe harbor I kept inside of myself was flooded with dread.

"They think that she took too many of her anxiety medications while drinking." He reached for my hand and managed to stop me right before I entered their room. "She's gone, Carson. There's nothing you can do."

She's gone. She's gone. My heart pounded to the beat of those words. Over and over again. It was the only thing I heard. It was the only thing I could feel as I jerked my hand from his and forced my way into their room.

There were even more people in here than there were in the entry of the house, and the sympathy on their faces felt like it was going to bury me alive. I pushed past them all, searching for her, and I didn't stop until I saw her lying on her bathroom floor.

I dropped to my knees beside her, and my hands trembled as I brought them up and pushed her hair out of her face. She looked so peaceful like she had simply fallen asleep for an afternoon nap, and my fingers tightened in her hair.

"Mom?"

I could hear talking behind me, but I didn't care what they had to say. I just wanted to hear her voice. I wanted her to blink her eyes open and tell me that everything was okay.

But she didn't.

She just lay there, and I couldn't stand it. I moved my hands to her shoulders, and I pressed my fingers into her skin as I shook her. "Mom!"

Someone's hand came down on my shoulder, but I

knocked them away. "Don't fucking touch me. Mom!" I screamed for her, but she didn't move. I screamed over and over, but that tranquil look on her face didn't budge.

"Carson." My dad was on his knees beside me, and I looked up at him and begged him with my eyes to make this stop. For once in his life, I just needed him to make this better. To make her better.

I begged him to take back everything he had ever done to her. I begged him to love her enough that he would have never broken her in the first place.

But he did none of those things.

He wrapped his arms around me, and I fought against him. But he didn't let me go. He refused to let me go until my body sagged against his and the tears began to fall from my cheeks. I fisted my hands into his shirt, and I held on to him for dear life.

I held on to him like he was the only thing I had left in this world, and he held me just as tightly.

"I love you." His whispered words were almost silent against my ear, but I heard them. I heard every word he said as he held me and kept my face turned away from her.

"She loved you so much."

"She's no longer in pain."

"You are the greatest thing that ever happened to us."

I heard them, but they were empty. I was completely and utterly empty.

"I can't do this." I pushed hard against his chest and stood on shaking feet. I looked down at my mother's body as I almost fell backward, then I forced my gaze away from her. Everyone was looking at me with sorrow and pity, and I hated every second of it. "I can't fucking do this."

I stormed past my mother, the smell of her floral perfume still clouding the air, and I stumbled outside until I reached my car.

Everything after that was a blur.

CHAPTER 15
ALLIE

My mom had been hammering me with questions for the last thirty minutes.

"So, does that mean the two of you are officially dating?"

"Oh my God, Mom. I told you it didn't." I screwed the lid onto my water bottle before unscrewing it again.

"But you like each other enough that you got matching tattoos?" She sipped her wine and leaned back in her chair to watch me.

"Trust me. I'm just as confused as you are," I said, exasperated by her questioning, but the truth was that I felt more clear than I ever had before.

"Well, where is Carson going to go to college when you graduate?"

My stomach felt like it was full of lead. "I don't know, but I think he's still planning on going to California."

"California?" My mom scrunched her nose up. "So, what would that mean? You two would do the whole long-distance thing? That would be really hard for such a young couple."

"Mom." I groaned and pressed my head against the kitchen table. "We're not even a couple. We had one good day together. That's it."

"What about sex?"

"Dear God," I whisper-shouted at her and stared down the hallway. "Can you please be quiet? I do not want Dad to hear you."

She rolled her eyes and took another sip of her wine. "It's almost midnight. Your dad has been snoring for hours. Plus, I'll just tell him everything later."

I groaned again just as my phone started vibrating on the table. I flipped it over and saw Josie's name. I would call her back. This conversation was something that I didn't want anyone to be privy to.

"You didn't answer my question."

"What was your question exactly?" My phone started buzzing again, and Josie's name flashed across the screen.

"Are you having sex with him? Are you being safe?"

I picked up my phone and stood from the table. "That's the second time Josie's called me. I really need to get this."

I hit Answer and pressed the phone to my ear as I headed toward my bedroom.

"This isn't over!" my mom yelled and I ducked into my bedroom before closing the door.

"Thank you." I sighed into the phone. "You know the perfect time to call."

"Allie." The pain in her voice put me immediately on alert.

"What's wrong?" I searched around my room as I waited for her answer. I slid my feet into my flip-flops and grabbed Carson's sweatshirt off my bed.

"It's Carson." Two little words and everything came

crashing down inside me.

"What do you mean? What happened?" I grabbed my keys from my desk, and I was already pushing out of my room before she answered again.

"It's his mom. It's bad, Allie. His mom overdosed."

"What?" No. No. No. No. This couldn't be happening. He was so happy today. Happier than I had seen him in so long that it had made my chest ache.

"Olly just called me. Apparently, it happened a couple hours ago, and it's so bad. Carson is out of control."

"Where is he?" I looked up at my mom, and she stood from the table in an instant. One look at me and she knew something was wrong. "Tell me where he is."

"Apparently there's a party at Joe's house tonight. Stay there, and I'll come get you."

"No." I shook my head even though she couldn't see me. "I can't just sit here that long. I'll meet you there."

I hung up the phone before she could refuse, and I tugged Carson's sweatshirt over my head.

"What's wrong?" My mom followed me to the front door as I tucked my phone into my front pocket.

"Carson needs me." It was the first thing I thought to say. It was the only thing I could feel. "Josie said that his mom overdosed tonight."

"Oh my God," my mom gasped, and my chest felt like it was cracking open. I knew Josie said that Carson was out of control, but I didn't know what that meant. I couldn't imagine what he must have been feeling or thinking. But I knew that none of it was good.

"I need to go, Mom." I was going to him whether she allowed it or not. "I have to get to him."

"Are you sure?" She looked hesitant to let me go as she

followed me out to the car. "They might need some time alone."

"No." He couldn't be alone right now. Not with the thoughts and fear and doubt that I knew had to be running through his head. Carson was his own worst enemy. He was as self-destructive as he was handsome, and I couldn't just sit here while I knew he was doing just that. "I need to be with him."

"Okay." She nodded and leaned against my door as I climbed into my car. "But please be careful and let me know as soon as you're with him."

"I will." I started the car and tried to pull my door closed. But she held it open.

"I love you, sunshine."

I could feel tears burning in the back of my eyes as I stared up at her. "I love you too."

...

I spotted Josie as soon as I climbed out of my car. She was chewing on her thumbnail as she paced the driveway.

"Where is he?" I asked as I passed her, already heading for the door.

"He's out back, but, Allie, you should prepare yourself."

I didn't know what that was supposed to mean, but I didn't have time to sit here and talk about it. Every part of me was dying to get to him. I needed to lay eyes on him to make sure he was okay. I need to run my hands over his skin and feel for myself that he was there.

Josie followed me as I pushed through the house. People were partying and drinking, and I hadn't thought twice about the fact that I was wearing nothing but a pair of tight pajama shorts and Carson's tank top. My hair was piled on the top of my head in a messy bun, and I didn't have a lick of makeup on my face, but I didn't care.

These people could think whatever they wanted about me. None of them mattered.

All that mattered was him.

I pushed through the back door and found him immediately. He was sitting back in a chair with a bottle of dark liquor in his hand, and he looked so broken. Even from so far away, I could see the pain and seething anger radiating from him, and when I looked over and noticed the girl who was sitting on his knee, all I could feel was sadness.

My chest ached and my hands shook as I moved toward him. He's hurt. I reminded myself that over and over as the girl ran her hand down his chest. I wanted to rip her off of him and demand answers from him, but that wasn't what he needed.

This was Carson coping; this was him pushing anything and everything away and clinging to the things he thought he could control.

I pushed through the sea of people until I was standing directly in front of him, and he leaned his head back against the back of the chair to stare up at me. There was a flash of pain in his eyes that made me feel like I was going to crumble into a million pieces, but I knew that I couldn't.

Not now.

"Hey, Allie." My name was lazy and slurred from his lips, and I hated the way it sounded.

"Hi." I tucked my hands into the pockets of my shorts and stared at him. I could feel the others watching us both, Beck and Olly both looked like they were on full alert, and I knew that I needed to tread carefully.

"What brings you out tonight?" He grinned, and it was so damn fake that it made my stomach turn. "I thought you were going home to get some sleep."

"I was." My gaze moved from him to the girl when she let her head fall back against his shoulder. My voice shook as I said the next words. "But I wanted to come see you. I wanted to check on you."

"I'm just peachy." He chuckled and brought the liquor bottle to his lips. It dribbled down his chin as he took a long pull of the alcohol, and it took everything inside me not to jerk the bottle from his hand.

"You don't look peachy."

He wiped at his chin with his hand that was still holding the bottle. "Don't I? Is there something wrong with my outfit?"

"Carson," I whispered his name because I didn't want to do this. I didn't want to fight against this ironclad wall he kept around him that he rarely ever dropped. I had to fight my way through it too many times before.

"What, Allie?"

"Don't do this. Can we go somewhere and talk?" I reached my hand out for him, but he just stared at it. There was so much emotion swirling in his eyes. He was so damn lost.

"No." He shook his head, and I watched as his hand moved around the waist of the girl on his lap and tightened. I could see his tattoo peeking out around the curve of his arm, and I wanted to rip it from her body.

Olly let out a curse, but I wasn't listening to him.

"I know you're hurt." I crossed my arms and tried my hardest not to do something irrational. "But if you don't get that girl off your lap right now, I'm going to do it myself."

The girl glanced up at me for the first time as if she hadn't even noticed me standing there.

"What are you going to do?" Carson cocked his head and a smile ghosted upon his lips.

"Whatever it is you force me to." I shrugged my shoulders. "Do you want me to fight her? Do I need to jerk her from your lap by her hair to prove that I care about you?"

The girl shifted on his lap, but his hand didn't budge.

"You wouldn't."

He was testing me, and I knew it. He was pushing me to walk away and turn my back on him because that's what he thought he deserved.

I closed the space between us, and my knee knocked against his as I stared down at the girl. She looked familiar to me, but I didn't know her. "Get off of him."

"What?" She laughed and looked back and forth between me and Carson, but he was still watching me.

"Get the fuck off of him." I reached forward to grab her hand, but she yanked it out of my touch. She stood from his lap, coming face to face with me, and even though I knew she did nothing wrong, I wanted to take every bit of anger I was feeling out on her face.

I knew that wouldn't help anyone, though, and she didn't deserve it.

"Come on, Carson. Let's get out of here."

"No." He chuckled and drank from the bottle again. "I'm exactly where I want to be."

My body pushed against the girl who was still standing there as I forced my way closer to him and took a seat in the spot she had just vacated. Carson was stiff beneath me, but I tried to not let it bother me.

Even though it did. It killed me inside.

He was hurt and broken, and he hadn't turned to me. He hadn't wanted to be with me when he should have needed me the most.

"What are you doing, Allie?" He grumbled behind me, and I turned in his lap until my side pressed against his chest.

I stared into his eyes, and I searched them for something. I had no idea what I was even looking for, but I was desperate for it. Just something that made me feel like I was making the right decision.

"If this is where you want to be, then this is where I'll stay." I shrugged and leaned into him further. His arm wrapped around my back, more out of necessity than want, but it still sparked something inside me.

"Go home." He shook his head. "I don't want you here."

His words sliced me open just as he had intended for them to do, but I didn't budge.

"Come home with me, and I'll leave."

"No." His answer was instant and reminded me of a storm. It was chaos and fear and the promise of destruction.

"Then I'm not leaving either."

He growled when my response wasn't what he wanted to hear, but I didn't care. There was no way I was going to leave him here like this. Especially when I knew that eventually this mask he was wearing right now was going to break, and when it did, I refused to let him face it alone.

"You never fucking listen." He huffed before bringing the bottle of liquor to his mouth again. I snatched it away before it could grace his lips.

His angry gaze snapped to mine, but I didn't waver. "Give that back to me, now."

"No." I shook my head and held it against my chest. "I think you've had enough."

"I'm not kidding, Allie. Fucking give it to me." He attempted to grab the bottle, but I held it out of his reach.

"It's not happening, Carson." I lifted the bottle and took a small drag of the liquor. It burned from the moment it touched my tongue all the way to my belly.

"What are you doing?"

"Getting drunk." I shrugged my shoulders and set the bottle on the ground by his feet. "If wasted is where you want to be, then I'll go there with you."

"Stop." His voice was commanding and hateful, and I could feel our friends watching us. They were watching him like they didn't trust a single move he made.

"What would you rather me do?" I leaned closer to him even though he tensed at the movement and pressed a gentle kiss to his jaw. He shuddered beneath my lips, but I didn't stop.

I wrapped my arm around his shoulder and turned in his lap until I was fully facing him. My legs rested on either side of his as I straddled his lap, and I didn't care who was watching us. I didn't give one thought to what any of them were thinking.

"Allie." He slammed his eyes shut and his hands rested on the sides of the chair as if they were careful not to touch me. "I can't do this tonight."

"I know." I ran my fingers down his neck, and his skin felt so hot beneath mine.

He opened his eyes and stared up at me with a lazy perusal, and even though he was angry, I still saw his raw lust staring back at me. He didn't stop me as I ran my fingers through his hair or over his bottom lip. He did nothing but stare at me while his Adam's apple shook with his deep swallow.

"I don't expect anything out of you, Carson." My voice was quiet and sounded much calmer than I felt inside. "I just want to be with you. I want you to let me take care of you."

He started to shake his head, but I pressed my palm into his cheek and stopped him. I leaned forward and pressed my mouth to his ear. "Please just let me love you."

He tensed beneath me, harder than before, and his hands immediately clung to my sides. His fingers dug into my skin, and I felt the bite of his pain under his touch.

"Stop." His voice shook, and I tightened my hold on him.

I wrapped my arm around his neck and buried my face in the opposite side. He did the same to me. His breath rushed in and out against my neck and his lips trembled against my skin.

"I'm so sorry, Carson. I'm so, so sorry."

He wrapped his arms completely around me, and he squeezed me tighter against him. "Oh, God." I barely heard his words before his body began to shake almost violently beneath me, but I didn't let him go.

I held on to him as he let go beneath me, and I tried to absorb every bit of pain I possibly could from him. My fingers tangled in the back of his hair, and I pressed small kisses to his neck as he fell apart. I tried to remind him that I was there, that he wasn't in this alone, and even though it hadn't been more than a handful of days since we were still hating each other, I knew that he would never be alone as long as I could help it.

Regardless of how he felt about me, I would love Carson Hale until I took my last breath and nothing that he did or said would ever take that away.

CHAPTER 16
CARSON

I felt like I was suffocating, and it had nothing to do with the fact that I was holding on to Allie so tightly that I feared she would disappear.

It was all too much. My mom. God, my mom. I still couldn't wrap my head around what happened or even comprehend that she was gone. It didn't feel real.

The urge to pick up my phone right now and call her was overwhelming. I just wanted to hear her voice and for her to tell me that everything was going to be okay.

I was desperate to know that everything was going to be okay.

I hadn't even been thinking when I left my house and raced as far away from it as I could get. I pulled up to the party without thought, and I had a bottle of liquor in my hand before anyone even realized I was there.

I had been alone for the first several minutes. It had felt like hours, honestly, but then I saw Beck and Olly storming through the back door with their eyes searching for me. And I knew that they knew.

The thing I was trying to hide from was now staring me directly in the face. The sympathy in their eyes was almost enough to kill me, and I quickly drank as much liquor as I could before they managed to get in front of me.

Neither of them had tried to force me to leave. They had asked, but when I said no, they simply sat beside me and watched me like I was going to break at any moment.

It wasn't until the moment when Allie stood in front of me that I thought I was going to fall apart completely. I couldn't stand to see her tonight. Not when everything seemed to be falling apart.

She looked so damn perfect standing in front of me, and I knew that she was. She was pure perfection, and every time I touched her, I tainted her with the fucked-up mess that I was.

Exactly like my dad had done with my mom.

I hated the look on her face when I tried to push her away, but I would rather see that than to see her become... fuck, I don't know. Broken. A shell. I didn't want Allie to be touched by the shit that affected me, and I hated that she was here to save me.

Because that's exactly what she was trying to do. She was trying to save me when I wasn't worth it.

But the moment she pressed her lips to my skin and asked me to let her love me, I knew that I couldn't let go. Even if she wanted me to, I would no longer be capable.

I clung to her as the tears fell from my eyes, and I hated that she was a witness to this. I despised the fact that she was the one having to hold me together while I completely fell apart.

And she did. She stayed there, with me clinging to her for dear life, while I cried and got everything out that I was holding inside. She didn't budge until I finally lifted my head to look up at her.

Those that had been around us were all gone, and I hadn't heard a single one of them leave. It was just me and her, and I felt a desperation for her that I didn't know I was capable of feeling.

"I need you." I pressed my mouth against hers, and she kissed me back as my hands roamed over her body.

"That's not a good idea." She shook her head, but she didn't stop kissing me.

"I don't care if it's a good idea or not. I need you." God, I sounded so frantic.

"Carson," she sighed against my lips. "You're drunk, and you've had an incredibly hard day."

"You are the only goddamn thing I care about right now." My hands pushed up my tank top that she was wearing until I felt her soft skin underneath. She let out the tiniest hiss at my touch, and that sound intoxicated me far more than any alcohol ever could.

"That's not true." She tried to disagree with me, but she was wrong.

"It is." I pressed my head against her chest, and she ran her fingers through my hair. "Please just let me disappear in you for a little while. Let me forget everything but your touch."

The way her breath trembled on her deep exhale was enough to do me in completely. This girl was hurting because she knew that I hurt. She was far too good for me, and we both knew it. But I was selfish enough not to care.

I needed her, and I felt like I wouldn't be able to breathe again if I didn't have her. If I didn't worship every inch of her skin.

Because she deserved to be worshipped. She deserved more than I could give her, but I wanted to try. I wanted to give her far more than my father ever gave to my mom. The thought of making sure that I never treated her like my father treated my mom was unwavering in my mind, but I knew that I had already done so much wrong.

This beautiful girl in front of me had already been so hurt by me. She was a fucking masterpiece, and I was ruining her.

She tugged on the strands of my hair and pulled my face up to meet hers. There was no hesitation as she brought her mouth to mine and kissed me. It felt every bit as desperate as I did. Her teeth ran over my lip before she sucked it into her mouth.

I moaned, and she swallowed the sound as she ground down against me. I was so damn hard beneath her, and my skin felt like it was set aflame.

My hands shook as they crept up her stomach and reached her breasts. She wasn't wearing a bra, and I groaned as I cupped her breasts in my hands.

"Oh my God." She jerked my hair even harder as she moaned against my mouth.

I pulled my mouth away from hers to kiss down her jaw and along her soft neck. I dropped one hand back down her body, and I slid my fingers beneath her shorts without an ounce of indecision.

She was already so wet, and I slid my fingers through her pussy as she moved against them. I slowly brought them back out and held my fingers between us before tasting her on my skin. Her gaze was transfixed on my mouth as I ran my tongue over my fingers, and I thought I was going to come in my pants when she leaned forward and tangled her tongue with mine.

She tasted herself on my fingers and my tongue, and she moaned as I slid all three fingers into her mouth and watched her suck them like she had that night with my cock.

Her tongue teased the tips of my fingers before she sucked them back into her mouth, and I squeezed her breast with my other hand as I watched her.

"God, I need to fuck you." I lifted my hips and tugged my shorts down until my cock popped out between us. Allie nodded her head as she still sucked on my fingers, and it was like she was somehow connected to every part of me.

The nip of her teeth sliced through my chest; the lap of her tongue felt like venom in my veins. She was slowly killing me, and I was desperately chasing the agony.

She lifted onto her knees, and I pulled her shorts and panties to the side. I dragged my fingers out of her mouth and slowly ran them down her chin, then to my cock. I pressed the head to her wet center, and she didn't give me the slightest moment before she lowered herself down onto me.

We groaned in unison as she stretched around me, and I fisted my hands into her bare thighs. She rode me at an almost frantic pace, and I stared up at her as I let her have that control.

She was so goddamn beautiful, and I could feel emotion thickening in my throat.

"Allie," I barely managed to say her name. She felt so damn good, like she was fucking made for me, and I knew that I would never find anyone like her again.

"Yeah?" She closed her eyes and leaned her head back. Her hands were buried in my chest as she continued to ride me, and her pussy clenched around me over and over. I knew that she was so damn close and so was I.

"Allie, baby. Look at me."

She did as I said, but she didn't quit moving against me. I wrapped my hand around the back of her neck and brought her mouth down to meet mine. I kissed her like I may never get the chance to again, and she whimpered in my mouth.

"Allie, I..." I hesitated because I knew this wasn't the right time. After everything that had happened today and everything we had been through, I should have just kept my damn mouth shut, but I couldn't. "I love you."

My words were whispered against her lips, and I wasn't sure if she heard them until she expelled a broken breath against my lips. She shook her head, but I tangled both my hands in her hair until I forced her to look directly at me.

I needed her to know. I needed her to believe what I was telling her even after all the fucking lies I had spewed over the past few years. "I've been in love with you for as long as I can remember."

Her breathing quickened and her thighs tightened around me.

"Carson, I..." Her eyes fluttered closed, and she was panting as she rode me.

My heart thundered in my chest, and I knew that I wouldn't last much longer. I felt like a caged animal, desperate for her words, her touch, desperate for anything other than this fucked-up mind of mine.

Her fingers tightened around my neck, and she pressed her forehead to mine as she cried out. She whimpered as I buried my fingers into her skin and thrust inside her as her pussy clenched around me.

"I love you too." Her whisper was so quiet I barely heard

it, but it pumped through my body like an antidote to every cruel fucking thought that ran through me.

I clung to her, her body impossibly close to mine, but still I needed more. I needed her closer. I didn't think about the pain my hands may have been causing her or the way she mewled against me as I chased my release. I was lost in the rush.

I came inside her with a growl that ripped from my chest, and I held onto her as if she would suddenly disappear. She didn't try to move out of my grip. She just held on to me as tightly as I was holding her, and I let everything else slip away.

CHAPTER 17
CARSON

My head was pounding in a way that made it almost impossible to open my eyes. I groaned and rolled to my side. I hit the body next to me and jerked.

I blinked my eyes open to find Allie lying next to me still fast asleep, and everything came rushing back to me. My mom, the party, the fucked-up way I had treated her while I was drowning in everything.

She should have left me there; she should have walked away and let me go under completely. That was what I deserved, but she didn't even consider it.

God.

I ran a trembling hand over her face and pushed her hair back to reveal the soft curve of her nose and the full arch of her lips. She looked so peaceful while she slept, so vacant of all the worries I knew constantly rolled through her head.

I didn't deserve her.

I had no idea what I was going to do or what was going to happen. I had no damn clue how I was going to go back into my house and live there without my mom. But I knew with certainty that I didn't deserve this girl in front of me.

More than that. I was bad for her. I would be her downfall just as my dad was for my mom. I would never forgive him for it, and she would never forgive me.

I pressed a kiss to her shoulder before leaning back and trying to ease out of the bed. I had just sat up when her hand reached out and grabbed ahold of mine. It wasn't gentle either. She was holding on to me like she knew exactly what was running through my head.

I looked ahead, staring around her bedroom, and tried to calm my heart that felt like it was already completely shattered. Her hand didn't loosen its grip. Not even for a second.

"Carson," she whispered my name, and it broke me more than anything ever could.

"I need to head home." I stood and forced her hand to fall from mine.

"Okay." She nodded and climbed to her knees on the bed. "I'll come with you."

"No."

She jerked back as if I slapped her.

"I just need some time to be alone. To clear my head."

She searched my face, and I knew that whatever she was looking for she wouldn't find. I was a fool to ever think that she would ever find it in me.

She visibly shuddered, and I hated the look that crossed her face before she stood. She blocked my path to her doorway, whether it was intentional or not. "If that's what you need, fine, but please don't push me away."

"I'm not." I lied to her, and we both knew it. She could see the truth in my eyes as clearly as I had been able to see it in hers last night when she told me that she loved me.

But us loving each other wasn't enough. We had both known exactly how badly I could hurt her, how much I had hurt her, and I knew that I would do it again. I would hurt her regardless of how badly I didn't want to.

It was what I did. Who I was.

"You did this before." She pushed forward toward me, and her hands clung to my shirt. I turned my head so I didn't have to face the heartache in her eyes. She refused to allow me that selfishness. She gripped my face in her hand and she forced me to look back at her. "I know what you're doing, and I won't let you."

"I'm not doing anything."

"Yes. You are!" she screamed at me, and her eyes filled with unshed tears. "You are doing what you always do. You push away the people you care about because you're scared."

I stared past her and tried to ignore her words. "I need to go check on my dad."

"You are not him."

My gaze snapped back to her, and I clenched my jaw.

"I know you, Carson, and I know that's exactly what you're thinking." Her hand in my shirt tightened to the point where I had no choice but to listen to her. "You blame him for what happened to your mom, but you are not him."

"I just..." I didn't know what to say. I didn't know how to explain the thoughts that were coursing through me like an echo. "I can't..."

"Go." She took a step back and moved out of my way. "If that's what you need to do, then go. But you are not going to push me away. You don't get to make that decision for me. Not again."

"Allie." I huffed, but she was already shaking her head.

"No. I love you, and I refuse to let you ruin this." A tear

streamed down her cheek as she stared at me. "Don't say anything you're going to regret."

I couldn't do this. Not today. I moved to walk past her without saying another word, but she stopped me again with her hand on mine.

"Please kiss me."

I knew that I shouldn't, but I couldn't stop myself. I leaned down until my lips met hers in a kiss that seared me. It burned me from the inside out, and I knew that I would never recover from her.

I kissed her until I couldn't take another second of it, then I walked out of her house and back to mine.

CHAPTER 18
ALLIE

I hadn't spoken to Carson in almost three full days.

I had been trying to give him space like he asked, but I hated it. I despised it because I knew that he was grieving and blaming himself for things he had no control over. I also knew that regardless of what I said, he was pushing me away.

"Are you ready to go in?" Frankie looked at me, and I could see the pity in her eyes. She knew it too.

They all did.

"Yeah." I straightened out my black dress and walked ahead of her toward the funeral home. "As ready as I'll ever be."

Josie caught up to me and wrapped her hand in mine before Frankie did the same on my left. I appreciated their support, the strength they were lending me, because I knew that I was going to have to be strong for Carson. Regardless of what he wanted, of how badly he tried to push me, he needed me now more than ever, and I would be there for him whether he liked it or not.

Beck and Olly were already inside. They had been with Carson all day, and I was thankful that they had been. I was relieved to know that they had him when I couldn't.

I took a deep breath as we reached the door and pushed inside. There were a ton of people mingling around the main reception area, some I recognized, most I didn't.

It felt suffocating. The heaviness, the grief, every bit of it was stifling, and I knew that Carson probably felt like a caged animal.

We walked through the crowd, and I felt like I couldn't breathe when I finally laid eyes on him. He stood next to his father in a solid black suit that was so similar to his dad's, but he looked so different. Carson held a cold indifference in his eyes while his dad shook hands and thanked people for coming.

If I didn't know him the way I did, I would have thought him almost completely unaffected by the whole thing, but there were so many signs of his grief. It was in the clench of his jaw, the way he drew his hand up into a fist before relaxing it again, but more than anything, it was the way he wouldn't meet anyone's eye. It was as if he feared that one single look would give him away.

We walked between the aisles, moving closer to him, and we were still at least a couple dozen feet away when he looked in our direction. Our gazes connected instantly as if he sensed me there, then he clamped them shut.

My hands trembled as I dropped my friend's hands and moved closer to him still. When he opened his eyes again, they were molten and filled with grief and anger and something I couldn't quite decipher. Unshed tears swam in his eyes as he stared at me, and I didn't know what to say to him. I had no idea what to do to help him.

But he didn't give me time to figure it out. Only a second after he opened his eyes, he left his father's side and pushed toward me. I watched him as he came, trying to prepare myself for what he would do, and I silently begged him not to push me away. Not today of all days.

But I knew that was likely. That was how Carson coped.

What I wasn't prepared for was for him to slam into me, wrapping his arms around me as he tugged me impossibly close. I held him to me even though we were in the middle of everyone and blocking the way. He didn't care and neither did I.

My throat was clogged with emotion, but it escaped me when his body shook against mine and he let out a strangled sob. I clung to him, pulling him closer and closer, clawing at his suit as the tears streamed down my cheeks.

I could feel people watching us, but I didn't care. They could think or say whatever they wanted. The only thing that mattered to me was him.

"I'm here," I whispered in his ear, and he shook harder.

I wasn't sure how long we stood there like that, but I knew it was long enough for Frankie to gently place her hand on my back. I pulled away from Carson, just slightly, and I saw the long line that had formed behind us.

Carson could see them too, but he had no concerns about them. His hands roamed over my face as if he was convincing himself that I was real, then he kissed me, long and hard, and my heart ached so much for my beautiful broken boy.

We moved out of the aisle, my hand in his, and he pulled me to the front with him. We sat down on the front pew, side by side, and I didn't let go of him for a single moment.

He wiped at his face, pushing away the tears that still fell, and I tightened my hand in his. He looked down at me before pressing another kiss against my lips. I wrapped my other hand around the back of his neck, and I held him there as I breathed him in.

"I love you," I whispered the only thing I knew to say.

"I love you too." He barely managed to choke out the words.

I looked down at our joined hands, and I ran my fingers over the spot where I knew his tattoo that matched mine marked his skin. Come what may.

Words that didn't hold nearly as much meaning when we had marked them on our skin.

He nodded his head as if he understood before kissing me on my forehead. Then he settled against me, and we stayed that way, hand in hand, as the service began and ended. And I refused to let him go as he said goodbye to his mother one last time. Even after, we were sealed together, and I didn't think I would be able to let him go.

CHAPTER 19
CARSON

I didn't know up from down.

Everything was fucked up. My mother was gone, buried in the dirt like she hadn't been everything to us once upon a time. I couldn't wrap my head around it. Nothing about it felt real.

And I was so fucking angry.

I could hardly see anything outside of my anger. Nothing but her.

I pushed Allie's hair out of her face and stared down at where her head rested on my chest. She had come home with me after the funeral without either of us saying a word, and she had stayed all night.

She didn't ask me to talk about anything or to apologize for the way I had treated her. She just held me and loved me, and fuck, she was far too good for me. I owed her all of that and more. I owed her everything, but I didn't know how to put into words what was racing through my head.

I tightened my arm around her, and she blinked up at me with the softest smile on her face.

"I'm sorry."

Her smile dropped suddenly, and she shook her head. "You don't need to apologize for anything, Carson. You've gone through so much."

I had, but she was wrong. "That doesn't excuse the way I treated you." I ran my fingers along her jaw. "I'm sorry for the way I reacted and for the way I pushed you away."

I closed my eyes against the sudden ache in my chest. "I've just been so fucked up in the head, and I don't want what happened to my mom to ever happen to you."

"Carson." She sat up fully with her hands on my chest and stared down at me. "That would never happen."

"I know." I nodded, because I did know. Those three days apart had taught me that. I watched my father plan the funeral and arrangements for a woman he didn't even love, at least not anymore, and I knew that Allie and I could never be anything like that. "I haven't felt like I was good enough for you in a very long time. Maybe not ever, and I still don't think I am."

She started to argue, but I slipped my fingers over her mouth to quiet her.

"But regardless of if I'm not good enough for you, I know that I will always love you. What my parents had, that wasn't love."

There was pure pity in her face reflecting back at me. "They loved each other."

"No. They didn't." I sat up in the bed and pulled her over my lap. Her thighs straddled mine, and she rested her hands on my shoulders. "My mom loved a man who hadn't loved her back in as long as I can remember. He didn't feel an ounce for her of what I feel for you."

"Carson." My name on her lips sounded like a plea for

me to stop, but I couldn't. Not until I told her exactly what I needed to say. For her to understand.

"That's the truth. I watched him while he was supposed to be grieving his wife, and I thought that I was doing the best thing by pushing you away. I didn't want you to be hurt by me ever again. I still don't. But I realized that..." I shook my head. "Shit, I don't even know what I'm trying to say."

"It's okay." She ran her fingers through my hair.

"I realized that I was more affected by pushing you away than he was by losing his wife," I said the thing I had been dreading saying out loud. "I will never do that to you, Allie. I will try to never hurt you again. I promise..."

"Hey." She pulled back on my hair and forced me to look up at her. My heart felt like it was going to beat out of my chest. "I know." She searched my eyes, and I had no idea what she was looking for. "I know that we have a lot of things we need to work on, but I also know that you love me. I know that we will never become them."

I tightened my fingers into her shirt and tugged her impossibly closer to me. "I do love you, you know. More than you'll ever know."

She pressed her forehead to mine and closed her eyes. "I love you too."

My hands shook against her because I knew that she loved me, but what I didn't know was if she really wanted this. After everything I had done to this beautiful girl, could she ever forgive me enough to give us a real chance?

"I want to be with you." My trembling hands snaked up her sides until they cupped her face. I pulled her away from me slightly until she was looking directly at me. My nerves felt like they were going to swallow me alive. "I know that I've fucked up over and over again, and I can't promise that I won't fuck up probably more times than we can count. But I still want to be with you. I know that might not be what you want, that you might never be able to forgive me, and that's okay. I'll do whatever it is…"

"I want to be with you too."

"You do?" My question sounded so damn pathetic and hopeful, but I didn't care. That was exactly how I felt.

She nodded her head in my hands. "I don't really think I have a choice. It's always been you."

I jerked her toward me in a rush and slammed my mouth against hers. Our kiss was impatient and messy and frantic.

"It's always been you too, Allie. Fuck. I've been such an asshole, but it's always been you."

She chuckled against my mouth and nodded her head. "You have been quite an asshole."

"But you still love me?"

"I do." She nipped at my lips, and I groaned. I felt that small bite all the way down to my cock. "I don't want you to lose all of that assholeness." She leaned back and there was a glimmer of teasing in her eyes. "It's kind of hot during sex."

"Oh yeah?" I flipped us over until she was on her back, and I was on top of her. Her giggles filled my room, and God, they sounded so good. "So, you want me to stay a part-time asshole?"

"Exactly." She leaned up enough to pull her shirt over her head. I stared down at her exposed breasts, and I didn't know what I did to ever deserve her. "You wouldn't be you if you didn't."

I leaned back on my knees and ran my hand down her body from her neck to just below her navel. "And which version of me do you want right now?"

She thrust her hips up against me, and she looked so fucking perfect.

"The real one." She put her hand on mine and pushed me further down her body. "I just want the version of you who can't get enough of me."

I ran my fingers over her pussy, and she mewled against the movement. "Ah, baby. You'll always have him."

CHAPTER 20
ALLIE

"You all have got to be the dumbest group of guys I have ever seen."

I snickered at Josie's comment and covered my mouth.

"Are you really going to let her talk to me like that?" Carson tugged on the edge of my t-shirt and pulled me toward him. My arms automatically wrapped around his neck, and I couldn't help laughing at the sour look on his face.

"Technically, she was talking to all of you like that. Plus, you all are being idiots."

He rolled his eyes, and I stared down at his bare chest. He was wearing nothing but his underwear, and if we weren't in front of all of our friends, I wouldn't have been able to keep my hands off him.

"We're just going surfing."

"In the freezing ocean."

"When it's freezing outside," Josie said almost at the same time as me.

Carson ignored both of our comments and pulled me

closer to him. "Also, it doesn't matter how she talks to them." He nodded toward Olly and Beck who were both inspecting their boards. "I'm your boyfriend. Not them."

"That still feels weird." I shook my head and ran my finger down the small indent in his chest.

"It feels right." He leaned forward and pressed a kiss to my forehead. My stomach tightened and my heart pounded. I didn't think I would ever get used to this, used to touching and showing affection so easily.

But that was exactly what was happening.

Ever since we left the funeral, Carson hadn't been able to take his eyes or his hands off of me. I knew that he was still working through so much in his head, in his heart, and he would be working through that for a long time. But I was more than willing to be here for him in the meantime, and if it meant that he wouldn't let me be more than five feet away from him, so be it.

I didn't want to be, anyway.

"You two need to get a room." Olly groaned as he looked at us.

"Don't be mad because you're the only one not getting it in." I smacked Carson's chest, but he still made a crude gesture with his body. Everyone laughed, but I could have sworn there was a look that passed between Olly and Frankie. It was fleeting and hidden, but I didn't miss it.

"Okay, sissies. It's time for you all to put your money where your mouth is. Get your asses in the water." Frankie stood from where she had been sitting in the sand and passed by Olly. She looked out toward the ocean before turning back to us. "I still think two out of the three of you will pussy out."

"Which two?" Beck moved next to his sister, and I watched him shiver in the cold air.

"You and Carson, obviously." She bumped his shoulder, and I laughed when they both scoffed.

Carson ran his nose along my neck and stopped with his mouth at my ear. "You want to come with me?"

"Not happening." I pushed against his chest, but he refused to let me go.

"Are you at least going to be here to get me warm when I get out?" He nipped my earlobe, and a chill ran up my spine.

"Maybe."

"You all have thirty seconds. You either swim out into the surf or you lose the bet and the three of you will have to streak at the championship game."

Carson let go of me then and all three of them grabbed their boards from the sand.

"How did we get into this again?" Carson mumbled to the boys, but we could still hear them.

"You, jackass. You don't know when to shut your mouth." Olly was the first one to touch the water, and he dove headfirst.

Beck and Carson followed after him, both hissing a string of curse words as they felt the water, and all I could do was laugh.

"We should just leave them and lock them out of the pool house." Josie laughed, and I took a seat in the sand. The two of them joined beside me as we watched the three guys swim out into the water.

"Thank you." I bumped my shoulder into Frankie's.

"For what?"

"For this." I nodded out to where the guys were now laughing. "For getting him out of his head for a little while."

"I think we should be thanking you for that." She squeezed my hand in hers. "I don't know that he would have been able to handle everything that's happened if it wasn't for you."

He would have. He would have probably handled it differently, but Carson was strong. He didn't need me to handle everything he did. He just needed time.

He still needed it, and he would continue to need it for a long time to come. But I would be by his side through it all.

"Ah. I didn't do anything besides..."

"Love him?" Josie looked over at me with a soft smile. "That's all you needed to do."

"Have you two talked about what you're going to do after graduation?" Frankie shifted more to look at me.

"Yeah. He's adamant that he's going to stay home now, but that's not going to happen. He's dreamed of going to the University of California with Olly forever, and that dream hasn't changed just because I'm in his life." I fidgeted with my sweater because even though that was truly what I wanted, the thought of him leaving made me panic.

"And you're going to stay here?" I couldn't tell if Josie was asking or just stating the fact, but I answered her anyway.

"Yes. We're going to be so far apart, but we'll figure it out."

Both of them nodded, but I could also see the hesitation and sympathy on their faces. They doubted if we could make it work. Hell, I did too, but I knew that I loved Carson and I would do whatever it took.

"Oh my God! There they go." Frankie pointed out to the water, and we watched as the three of them paddled their boards side by side and chased a wave.

"What about you? How are you going to feel when Olly leaves?"

Frankie blushed and tucked her dark hair behind her ear. "I mean, I'll be sad that my friend's leaving, but it will be the same with Carson. I don't even remember life without them in it."

"But it's different." Josie grinned.

"No. It's not." Frankie shook her head, and I felt so sorry for her.

"So, there's nothing going on between you and Olly?" I asked hesitantly. I didn't want to push her on the subject, but I also wanted one of my best friends to know that she could talk to us about anything. "We all see the way the two of you look at each other."

"You mean the way I look at him." She rolled her eyes and huffed. "I'm pretty sure Olly only hangs around me because he thinks he's my guard dog. He doesn't want anything to happen to me, no one to touch me, but trust me when I tell you that he won't touch me either."

"Have you tried?" Josie leaned in even closer.

"Yes." Frankie was messing with her fingers in front of her. "I've tried an embarrassing amount of times, and every single time, he has shot me down. I think what happened with Lucas really fucked with his head. Like, more than the other guys'." She looked up at us, and there was so much sadness hidden in her dark brown eyes. "If he ever considered anything between us before, he definitely won't now."

"That's stupid." Josie growled. "The two of you would be perfect together."

She nodded as if she thought so too. "But could you imagine Beck? This isn't just his friend hooking up with his sister. He has reason to be overprotective, and he trusts Olly and Carson more than anything in the world. If he found out something happened between us, he would hate Olly."

"He would get over it."

"Would he?" she asked, and I knew that she had considered that question at least a hundred times before. "Olly doesn't think so."

"Well, then we have to find you someone else," Josie said as she squared her shoulders. "Make Olly realize everything he's missing."

"That's just it." Her voice shook, and she looked out at the water where the boys were now surfing toward us. We missed the whole thing while we were talking. "I don't think he's missing out on anything. He's just not as loud about it as Carson was. Oh shit. Sorry."

"Don't be." I shook my head, but there was a sting of jealousy that hit my chest.

"But I still think he's got plenty of girls to choose from. I don't think he's missing out on anything by not wanting me."

"He may not be willing to cross that line, but he wants you." I reached forward and held her hand in mine. "Nobody looks at a girl like that they don't want."

I felt the cold drops of water before I looked up and saw Carson standing over me. "What who wants?"

"Nothing." The three of us answered in unison, and Carson narrowed his eyes.

"Did you all even watch us surf in that freezing cold water? That was impressive."

"What's impressive is that you had very minimal shrinkage." Frankie pointed to Carson's very obvious dick outline that was staring me right in the face, and all three of us fell over in a fit of giggles.

"What's so funny?" Beck pushed his hair out of his face as he and Olly made their way up the beach to us.

"One. They didn't even watch us. Two." Carson covered

his package with his hands as if he just thought of it. "Your sister just complimented me on my lack of shrinkage."

I watched as a glimmer of jealousy flashed in Olly's eyes, but he hid it just as quickly.

"That's disgusting, Frankie." Beck sat down next to Josie and pulled her into his wet body even as she laughed and tried to knock him away.

"What about you?" Carson nodded down in my direction. "Are you impressed by my stamina even in the freezing cold water?"

I smiled up at him and shrugged my shoulders. "I've seen better." I barely got the words out before he scooped down and threw me over his shoulder.

"We'll see about that."

I laughed as my chest hit his back and the only thing I could see was his wet ass and the sand. "Put me down. You're wet!"

"And you're about to be."

I smacked him because I could hear our friends laughing behind us, but he didn't stop.

He pushed through the Clermonts' back gate, and I watched upside down as we passed by the pool. "Carson, put me down."

"Not happening," he growled, and I wiggled against him in an attempt to push myself up. That did nothing but get my ass smacked as he stormed into the house. I prayed that Mr. and Mrs. Clermont hadn't come home while we were down at the beach because I would be absolutely mortified if they saw me.

Luckily, we didn't see anyone as he climbed up the stairs two at a time, and I clung to his middle as I hoped he didn't drop me. We passed by Beck's door and pushed into the guest room where he normally stayed.

He tossed me down onto the bed, and I looked up at him. He was so damn handsome. He was wearing nothing but his black underwear and his light hair was disheveled from the ocean, but every single inch of him was so tempting.

"You've seen better, huh?" He gripped my ankle in his hand before tugging me to the end of the bed.

"That was a joke." I laughed, but he was already tugging my shoes from my feet and tossing them across the room. He didn't hesitate for a second before his fingers met the top of my yoga pants, and he pulled them down my legs.

"You weren't very impressed?" He raised an eyebrow and ran his thumb down the center of my panties.

"I didn't say that!"

"You insinuated it." He cocked his head to the side and watched his hand, and I squirmed beneath his touch.

"You did just go out and surf in the freezing water. That isn't very impressive."

His gaze snapped up to mine, and a wicked smile lit up his face.

"I guess I'll have to try harder then, won't I?" He didn't give me time to respond. He tugged me further down the bed until my ass was barely on the edge, and he dropped to his knees between my thighs. I bit my lip as I watched him and tried to calm the building tightness that was already forming in my belly.

His fingers snaked into the sides of my panties, and I held my breath as I prepared for him to tug them down my legs. It didn't matter how many times he did this. I would never get used to this beautiful boy kneeling between my thighs and preparing to worship me.

It felt like a dream that I never wanted to wake up from.

His hands jerked harshly against my hips, and I heard the ripping of fabric before I felt my panties fall away from my skin.

"Oh, God."

He ran his tongue through my pussy, not giving me a single moment to prepare myself, and I felt like I was already about to fall apart around him.

"You're so fucking wet, baby." His words were mumbled against my skin.

His mouth was rushed, his tongue adept, his teeth teasing. I pushed my fingers into his hair and held him against me as I raised my feet to rest on his shoulders. He groaned before pressing his palms into my thighs and spreading them as wide as they would possibly go.

He left his hands there, holding me in place, but I still tried to buck against his mouth. I was desperate for everything he was giving me, and I was chasing every second of it.

He sucked my clit into his mouth, and my back bowed off the bed. I was going to come. That quickly under his touch, I was going to completely lose myself in him.

"Are you impressed?" His whisper was so low I barely heard him.

"What?" I pushed his head harder against me, but he didn't budge. He held himself exactly where he was as he looked up at me patiently.

"I said, are you impressed?" He grinned and pressed the softest kiss to my center. My hips jolted forward, but his hands kept them in place.

"Yes, yes. God, yes. Is that what you needed to hear?" I was scrambling to give him whatever he wanted because I felt like I was going to die if he didn't touch me again.

"It's a start." He smiled that devilish smile of his before he sucked my clit back into his mouth and threw me over the edge. I pulled his hair in my hands as my orgasm racked through me, and I didn't even realize I was screaming until his hand pressed against my mouth.

He moved over me, kissing every inch of skin he passed, before his mouth replaced his hand against my lips. His palm wrapped around my thigh, and he lifted it to wrap around his naked hip after removing his underwear.

He sat up onto his knees and stared down at my pussy as he ran his length up and down my wetness. Over and over, he moved himself against my most sensitive parts until I was a squirming mess beneath him.

"Carson, please." I hooked my other leg around him and tried to force his hips toward me.

"Tell me how impressive I am." He grinned up at me, and I knew that he was just toying with me now.

I huffed and sat up enough to push against his chest. "You have got to be the most egotistical jerk I have ever..."

He pushed inside me then and the rest of my words fell from my lips. I dropped back to the bed, and his body chased mine before he pushed my shirt and bra up my body and his tongue met my nipple. He teased and kissed and nipped as he slid in and out of me, and I could feel my orgasm building again.

"Yeah, but you love this egotistical jerk." He ran his tongue up the center of my chest before moving to my neck. "Right?"

These were the two sides of Carson that were so vastly different. The teasing playboy and the vulnerable lover. My need for both was overwhelming.

"You know that I do."

"Tell me." He buried his face in my neck and moved inside me in a way that made me forget my own name let alone what he was talking about.

"I love you." I moved my hips against his as he pumped into me. Both of us were beyond gentle touches and teasing caresses. We were desperate for each other, and nothing could stop us.

He pulled my knees higher, changing the angle and hitting a spot inside me that had me crying out. "I love you too," he groaned, and he didn't stop until both of us were panting messes, slick with sweat.

He laid down next to me and pulled me closer to him until my body was half covering his. He pressed a gentle kiss to my forehead before he smacked my bare ass. "Don't forget it either."

CHAPTER 21
CARSON

"Are we really doing this?" Allie grumbled, and I laughed.

"Yes. You're the one who brought it up."

"I know, but I feel silly now." She shook her head and a few strands of her sun-glistened hair fell free.

"Why?"

"None of our friends are here."

"So?" I pulled her closer to me and her dress whirled around her. "We don't need our friends to have a good time together."

"I know, but..." She looked to her school, then back to me.

"Do you not want to show me off at your homecoming dance?" I teased her.

"Of course, I do. Look at you." She waved her hand to my suit.

"Then come on." I tugged her hand and led her into the school. It looked so vastly different than Clermont Prep, and I tried to imagine Allie here day in and day out.

I handed our tickets to the teacher who was perched behind an old folding table before we pushed through the doors to the gymnasium. It was decorated in an assortment of streamers and balloons, and a large disco ball hung from the ceiling.

"This is awesome." I pulled Allie into me, and she giggled.

She looked nervous for whatever reason, but I wouldn't let her fall into that. I gripped her hand in mine and twirled her around until the two of us landed on the dance floor. There was barely anyone dancing, but that didn't stop me.

I pulled her body against mine and held her hand to my chest as the other pressed against the small of her back.

"Do you think I'll get homecoming king?" I looked around the room and there were so many envious eyes staring at me. So many guys who had lost their chance with this girl in my arms.

"You can't." She rolled her eyes. "You don't even go here."

"Maybe they'll make an exception considering we are by far the most beautiful couple here."

"Oh my God." She let her head fall onto my shoulder. "Sometimes I forget how full of yourself you are, but you're always there to remind me."

"You're welcome." I laughed and spun her around.

She smiled up at me, and I swore there was nothing more beautiful in the world. It was a smile she had given me every day, both of us insanely happy, and it was almost enough to make me forget all the fucked-up shit that had happened.

But nothing would ever be able to heal the wound of losing my mother, and nothing anyone said would ever change the fact that I blamed my father.

He may not have held the bottle of liquor or the pills to her mouth, but he was the reason she had relied on either to get through her day. He broke her long before her death, and we both knew it.

It was the reason he barely showed his face back at the house, a place that felt like it was nothing more than a haunted memory.

Part of me couldn't wait to leave but the other part of me was so damn conflicted. Allie had encouraged me to go to the University of California after graduation; that regardless of how far apart we would be, we would make it work.

But the thought of being that far from her felt impossible. Nothing was as important as her. Not school, not baseball, nothing.

But she thought I was crazy.

"This is actually kind of lame." Allie looked around and hugged me tighter.

"Well, we could always go find an empty classroom and make our mark on this place." I joked, but her eyes sparked with mischief.

"Do you think we would get caught?"

"I don't know." I ran my nose along her jaw. "Do you think you can keep quiet?"

"Maybe." She shrugged her shoulders and ran her fingers over my lips. "I could at least try."

"Don't fuck with me, baby." I nipped at the tip of her finger. "I will fuck you all over this school if you aren't careful."

That didn't deter her at all. Her eyes darkened and her breath caught in her throat.

"I'm not joking," she whispered, and that was all I needed.

I pulled her out of the gymnasium, back in the direction we came, and I led us toward the open bathrooms. There were a few teachers mingling around, and they paid us attention only long enough to see where we were going.

When they began talking again, we slipped down the adjacent hallway in a fit of laughter.

"Shh." I held my finger to her mouth as I pushed her against a set of red lockers.

"Make me," she murmured, and I quieted her with my mouth on hers. She tangled her fingers in my hair, tugging on the ends, as she kissed me.

She looked so damn beautiful tonight, her hair perfectly in place, her lilac dress fitted against her body before flowing freely from her waist to her knees. She was almost too damn lovely to damage, but the idea of marking her, of ruining her with my touch, overpowered everything else.

"Which classroom, baby?" I didn't stop kissing her as I asked my question, and she only pulled away long enough to nod down the hall.

I lifted her in my arms, my hands cupping beneath her ass, and moved us down the hallway. She wrapped her arms around my shoulders as she bounced against me, and her cleavage was so damn enticing that I almost tripped over my feet.

"Carson," Allie hissed on a laugh, and I straightened us.

I pushed her back against the first classroom door we came to, but the damn thing was locked. "Fuck."

Allie laughed again and I shh'd her. "You're going to get us caught before we even get started."

We tried the next door and that one was locked too. I growled as I powered across the hallway and reached for the next handle I could find.

Thank God that one opened, and I quickly shut it behind us as we entered the dark room. I didn't take the time to look around or come up with the best plan. I set her down on the first desk I saw, the teacher's desk, and I loosened the black tie that was around my neck.

I reached for her, and she was already pulling her dress up her hips. I groaned deep and loud when I saw that she wore nothing beneath.

"Goddamn, Allie. Are you trying to kill me?" I quickly undid my belt and the button of my pants before the loud sound of my zipper echoed through the room.

"Fuck me, Carson." She leaned back onto her elbow before her other hand reached between her thighs. "I'm so wet."

I gripped her thighs and tugged her further down the desk until she was perfectly lined up with me. "This is going to be quick." I rubbed myself up and down her wetness. "I've been thinking about stripping you out of that dress from the moment you put it on."

She whimpered as I skimmed over her clit, and the sound drove me wild. I pushed inside her, and she was so damn tight that I felt like I could come already.

Allie didn't hesitate as she rotated her fingers in the smallest circles against her clit, and I moved inside her at a matching speed.

"Oh, God." She slammed her head back against the desk and wrapped her legs around my back. She rode me as I slammed into her.

"Carson," she screamed my name, and I covered her mouth with mine. "Shh. I don't want to get this pretty ass expelled."

"Harder," she moaned again and didn't pay any attention to my warning.

So, I did what she said. I fucked her and fucked her, and I didn't stop until I felt her come on my cock and only then did I let go. I came with a roar and pressed my forehead against her chest.

We stayed there for several minutes until we caught our breath, then she straightened her dress while I worked on my suit.

"Well." I grinned down at her and pressed my hands onto the desk on either side of her hips. "Was coming to homecoming worth it?"

"Yeah." She nodded and pushed her curls out of her face. "Even if I didn't end up with the homecoming king."

I lifted her off the desk and she squealed in laughter, and I promised myself that I would force her to make that sound as often as I possibly could.

Our futures were uncertain, but I knew that I would be desperate for that sound regardless of where our lives took us.

I threw her over my shoulder and my hand came down on her ass as I moved us out of the classroom.

"Put me down." She laughed but I continued to truck ahead.

"Not happening, baby. You're mine."

"People will see us." She shrieked but there was still so much laughter in the sound.

"I don't care."

"Carson Hale, you are the devil."

I slapped her ass again before I rubbed my hand over the silky fabric. "Yeah, but I'm your devil."

EPILOGUE
ALLIE

One Year Later

I stood just outside of the locker room and waited.

I hadn't seen Carson in person in months, and I was dying to just push through that damn door and find him. But he didn't know I was here.

It was his birthday weekend, and I had told him that I couldn't get away because I was behind on a project for my psychology class. How he ever believed I would actually be behind on schoolwork was beyond me, but he had. He had been pouting for weeks now.

He didn't know that I had been here for his entire game or that I sat up in the bleachers drooling over how incredibly hot he was. He had played better than I had ever seen him play before. This was what he was meant to do, and I was so damn happy that I had finally convinced him to keep his scholarship to the University of California instead of staying home in Clermont Bay with me like he wanted to.

He would have never had this there, and he would have eventually regretted it.

Olly walked out of the locker room, and a grin lit up his face when he saw me. He looked handsome, far more so than I remembered, and I knew it had everything to do with the light scruff on his face and the way he was letting his hair grow.

"Well, aren't you a sight for sore eyes?"

"He still in there?" I nodded to the locker room.

"He is." He nodded. "He's probably beating off in the shower to thoughts of you since you left him stranded this weekend."

I couldn't stop the laugh that bubbled up my throat.

"Frankie come with you?" He looked to the locker room door then back to me.

"No." I shook my head. "She couldn't get away." It was a lie, and we both knew it. I didn't know what had happened between them, but Frankie hadn't wanted to come with me for a visit in a while.

Olly nodded as he opened the locker room door and yelled inside. "Carson, you have a package out here!"

"What is it?" I heard his voice, and the butterflies that were already fluttering around my stomach took full flight.

"How the fuck am I supposed to know?"

I could hear Carson grumbling, but Olly closed the door and winked at me before moving further down the hall.

"Well, where the hell is it?" The door opened and Carson looked right outside the door. He was wearing nothing but a pair of sweatpants and his tennis shoes. His hair was still wet from the shower and a drop of water fell down his torso.

"Right here."

His gaze snapped up to me as soon as he heard my voice,

and there was only a second of thought before he charged across the hallway to where I stood. He gripped my thighs in his hands and lifted me in the air. I wrapped my legs around his back just as mine hit the wall.

"What are you doing here?" he asked just before he kissed me.

"I wanted to surprise you." I giggled as his mouth ran over my face, my jaw, across my lips.

"Well, I'm definitely surprised. I've been a grumpy motherfucker thinking you weren't going to be here."

I couldn't stop laughing. "Olly told me something like that."

He shook his head against me with a chuckle. "Of course, he did."

His hands gripped my ass, and he pulled me tighter against him. I could feel his erection pressing into me, and I couldn't stop myself from grinding my hips into him.

"Fuck, we're not going to make it back to my dorm." He kissed my neck again just as several of his teammates pushed out of the locker room.

There were a slew of whistles and lewd comments, but I didn't care. I was finally in Carson's arms after being apart, and I didn't care who saw us.

"Keep it moving." Carson waved them on, but they continued to tease him as they walked.

"Oh, Allie!"

"Fuck, I miss Allie."

"I need to call Allie. I need to jerk off to a picture of Allie."

"Okay, assholes," Carson growled, but I was laughing in his arms.

"We're so glad you're here, Allie," one of his teammates

said as they walked away. "He's been an even bigger ass lately than normal lately."

"Ignore them." He shook his head and kissed me again.

"Have you missed me, Carson Hale?" I teased.

"God, you know I have." He pushed us off the wall, and I had no idea where we were going until he pushed through the locker room door. There were still a few guys gathering their things, but they all grinned and made their way out the door when they saw us.

"What are you doing?" I whispered and held onto Carson's shoulders. "Take me back to the dorm, or hell, your car."

"Can't." He shook his head and pressed my back against a set of lockers. "I need you."

I didn't argue. My heart was hammering in my chest, and I needed him too. He dropped me to my feet and used his hands on my hips to spin me around. I pressed my hands against the lockers as I heard his, "Oh fuck. You're wearing my jersey?"

He jerked my shorts down my legs in a rush, and I prayed that all of his teammates were long gone. But I didn't stop him. I wanted him just as badly as he wanted me. I needed him.

My panties came down next, and I moaned as I felt him drop to his knees behind me. He gave me no time to prepare myself before his mouth met my skin, and I felt his tongue roll through my pussy.

"Oh, God." My forehead hit the locker with a loud crash, and Carson only forced his tongue against me harder.

He lifted my leg, pulling my shorts and panties off my foot, then he spread my legs and forced my hips further back.

"God, how do you taste better than I even remember?" He moaned before diving back into me.

I held onto the locker and tried to convince my trembling legs not to buckle. It had been so long since I had seen him, touched him, since he had touched me, and my body was as desperate for him as I was.

"Carson."

His fingers met his tongue, and together they worked me until I was nothing but a mess. His fingers pinched down on my clit as his tongue pushed inside me, and I came so hard against his mouth that I knew anyone within the vicinity would hear me scream.

Carson moved behind me and his hands moved around my hips. My legs were still trembling, and I couldn't calm my racing heart even if I wanted to. "Hold on, baby. I need to fuck you."

I pressed my hands harder into the locker as he pulled my hips further toward him, and we both moaned when he finally sank inside of me.

He pushed into me, and with every thrust, he uttered words against my skin.

"I've missed you so fucking much." His tongue ran over the back of my neck.

"You're so damn gorgeous." A kiss to my shoulder blades.

"God, I love you." His tongue along my spine.

"I love you too," I managed to say around a moan as Carson's hand found my clit.

He thrust into me, hard, relentless, desperate, as his hand kept pace against me, and I was already falling apart for a second time.

"Carson," I called his name, and his other hand tightened around my ass.

"I'll never get enough of you." He came inside of me, and I chased him over the edge. He held me against him as my orgasm raced through me, overpowering my every thought, and I was drowning in everything that was him, his scent, his touch, his kiss.

He sat on the bench and cradled me in his lap. My body was so relaxed that I barely had the energy to lift my head and look at him.

His breath rushed in and out of him, and he pressed his hand against my chin to bring my mouth to his. He kissed me, slow and delicious. "I'm so glad you're here."

"Me too." I nodded against him. "Especially if this is the kind of welcome I get."

He chuckled against my neck and wrapped his arms around my middle. "Did you expect anything else?"

"With you? No." I shook my head as he laughed.

"Let's get you dressed so I can take you back to my dorm."

"Can I make a request?" I turned more in his lap to look at him.

"Anything." He breathed the word, and I knew that he meant it. After the last year, I knew without a doubt that he would do any and everything for me. For us.

"Bring home the uniform." I nodded toward the locker.

"Oh, yeah?" He chuckled as I stood and pulled my panties and shorts up my legs.

"Yeah." I nodded and bit my lip as I stared at him. He was so gorgeous, and he was all mine.

"Anything for you."

PROLOGUE
OLLY

Two Years Earlier

God, she was so pretty.

I clenched my hand at my side to avoid reaching out and touching her.

She was also too young for me and she was my best friend's little sister, but neither of those things seemed to matter when I was looking at her.

I was always looking at her, but she was looking at him.

Lucas grinned at her from across the table, and a soft blush bloomed across her cheeks. He was one of my best friends too, but I wanted to kill him when he looked at her like that. My stomach hardened as I watched them. I knew I didn't have the right. She wasn't mine, but for some reason, she felt like it.

She had felt like it for far longer than I liked to admit.

"What are you up to today, Frankie?"

She pulled her attention away from Lucas long enough

to look over at me. "Not a whole lot. I thought I might go for a swim before the party tonight. You're going, right?"

"Yeah." I nodded. "I'll be there."

"Good." She smiled at me as she leaned against her hand. "What about you, Lucas? Are you going to be there?"

I clenched my teeth as I waited for his response. He always treated Frankie as if she wasn't important. He treated her like she wasn't the most important person in the room even though she looked at him like he was the most crucial thing in her life.

"Of course." He rubbed his hands together as he talked, but he was barely looking at her. "I need to get fucked up or laid tonight."

Frankie's shoulder slumped the smallest bit, and she looked away before either of us could see her face.

A face I knew she was attempting to school to hide her hurt.

"Real classy, Lucas." I rolled my eyes because even though I had been friends with Lucas for what felt like forever, I still didn't see what Frankie saw in him. I was beginning to wonder why I was friends with him at all. "Come on, Frankie. Let's go hit the beach before the party."

"Okay." She nodded and stood from her seat. "Let me grab my suit."

As soon as she left the kitchen, Lucas leaned back in his chair and chuckled.

"What the fuck is wrong with you?" I glared at him.

"What's wrong with you?" He laughed harder. "You look like a lovesick puppy over Beck's little sister when you can get any pussy you want in the entire school. Don't let a piece of ass make you look so pathetic."

"Don't fucking talk about her like that." My pulse was

racing as I clenched my fists at my sides. "You have no idea…"

"What are you assholes talking about?" Beck interrupted us as he walked into the kitchen and grabbed an apple off the island.

"Trying to get Olly laid." Lucas smirked, and my fingers tingled with the urge to knock it off his face.

"It's about damn time." Beck wrapped an arm over my shoulder and laughed. "You've been a little tense."

"Fuck you both." I shrugged Beck off me just as Frankie came back around the corner. She was wearing a simple black bikini, but I couldn't look away.

"Hey, you ready?" She held a towel against her stomach, and I watched as her eyes flashed over to Lucas before looking back at me.

"Yeah. Let's go." I opened the back door and waited for her to walk through. This was Frankie's house, but I felt like I knew it as well as my own. I practically lived here most days.

Frankie walked in front of me, and I stared at the soft slope of her back as she pushed through the back gate and out onto the sand.

"Is it just me, or does Lucas seem like he's in a bad mood?" She looked back over her shoulder at me. She pushed her hair out of her face before looking back down at the sand.

"He's just being a dick." I pulled my t-shirt over my head and tossed it down. "Don't let him bother you."

"I'm not." She looked back to the house, and we both knew she was lying. She tossed her towel down on top of my shirt, then followed me into the ocean. "I just don't like when any of you are upset. Speaking of, did your dad show up to your game last night? I didn't see him."

"No." I laughed it off because Frankie and I both knew that wasn't something I wanted to talk about. "He had to work."

He always had to work. Him and my mom both.

But don't change the subject on me. We both know you like Lucas, and we also both know that he's not the guy for you.

I was. I didn't dare say that out loud. I shouldn't have been thinking about my best friend's little sister at all, but the idea of her doing anything with Lucas made me feel irrational.

"You don't know that." Her jaw clenched as she turned toward me. "What's going on with you two, anyway? You're supposed to be friends."

"We are friends." I ran my wet hand through my hair and pushed the thick strands back out of my face. "And I know him better than you do. Trust me when I tell you that you deserve better."

I knew what kind of asshole it made me to be talking about my friend like this, but I saw the way he treated girls. They were nothing more than easy fucks or a leg up in some way.

He was just like his stepdad, and there was no way in hell I was going to allow him to use Frankie in either of those ways.

I knew Beck wouldn't either. Hell, Beck would probably kill me if he had any fucking clue of the inappropriate thoughts I had about his sister, but Beck didn't see Lucas the way I did.

He didn't see the way he acted around Frankie because he never did it in front of him.

But I saw everything when it came to her.

"I think you think too highly of me, Olly." She sank into the water, and I watched as the water rolled over her shoulders.

"No. You just think too little." Shit. That came out wrong. She chuckled and splashed some water at my chest. "You know what I mean. You don't see you the way I see you."

Her head cocked to the side as she studied me, and I shifted on my feet. She was within arm's reach of me, and I could have easily pulled her toward me and tasted her lips that had been haunting me.

"And how do you see me, Olly?" She swam closer to me, and the gentle waves of the ocean felt like they were suddenly beating against me.

"I…" *God, were her eyes always that dark?* "I…"

"Frankie! Mom wants you!" The sound of Beck's voice made me jerk back away from her even though there was still plenty of distance.

Frankie blinked, and I could have sworn she was looking at me differently than she was only moments before. This girl was fucking with my head.

Maybe Lucas was right. Maybe I did need to get laid.

But when I closed my eyes and held my cock in my hand, she was all I could think about. I had never been so screwed up over a girl, but why did it have to be her?

Lucas was right when he said I could have had almost any girl in school that I wanted, but I couldn't seem to force myself to want any of them. And trust me, I desperately wanted to.

I would have given anything to stop wanting Frankie the way I did.

"I'm coming!" Frankie yelled back to Beck, but she was still looking at me.

I felt like I could barely breathe as she watched me, her dark brown eyes flicking back and forth between mine, and I had no idea what she was searching for.

But I would have given it to her.

If only she was looking at me like she looked at him. I would have given her anything.

"You should head in. I'm going to swim for a bit and clear my head."

"Okay." She nodded and hesitated only for a second before she headed out of the water. "We'll talk about this later, though?"

"Of course." I smiled at her and rubbed the back of my neck.

But I never should have let her go.

CHAPTER 1
FRANKIE

Two Years Later

Summer was just about to begin, but the water was still freezing. It nipped at my ankles as I slowly pushed through the sand and forced myself into the ocean.

"Come on." Olly reached his hand out for me and grinned. He had already dived headfirst into the water, and his wet, brown hair was pushed back out of his eyes.

Did he have to be so damn handsome?

"It's cold." I wrapped my arms around my chest, and his gaze fell there as if that one simple movement was a magnet. Goose bumps broke out across my skin, and I told myself that it was simply from the water and had nothing to do with the way my friend was looking at me.

"Don't be a chicken, Frankie. It's not that bad." He stepped closer to me, and there was a spark of mischief in his eyes that made my heart race.

"No!" I squealed just as his arms wrapped around my middle, and he lifted me onto his shoulder.

I didn't want to be thrown in that damn cold water, but God, it felt so good to have his arms wrapped around me. To feel his skin pressed against mine.

It made me feel like I was suddenly on fire, and only he could stifle the flames that felt like they were devouring me.

How someone could have so much power over me without even trying was pathetic.

It was more than pathetic honestly, but I also couldn't bring myself to care. Every moment that I got to spend with him fueled me. It made me want him more even though I knew that was the last freaking thing that should happen between us.

If Beck hadn't wanted me to date one of his friends before, Lucas had obliterated that option with everything he did to me. To them.

Pain sliced through my chest at the thought, and my body tensed against Olly. He noticed it immediately, and I could feel the tension in his own frame.

Of course, he noticed.

He noticed everything, and he could always see through me so easily.

He read my body so effortlessly, and most of the time, I felt like he could read my mind too. That was what worried me the most because he had to know. He had to realize exactly what I felt for him.

Because even though I tried to hide it, I didn't stand a chance.

I felt like everything about me was screaming how badly I wanted him, how desperately I needed him. Olly knew. He had to. Even if he tried to act like he didn't. Even if he tried to pretend like we were the happiest little friends who had nothing else going on between us.

He was a fool, and so was Beck if he didn't see it.

We all were.

Olly slowly lowered me down against his body into the water instead of throwing me, and I was hyperaware of every inch of my skin that touched his.

His brows were drawn together, and I couldn't miss the way he clenched his jaw as he looked me over.

For once, I just wanted to be any other girl that he wanted. I hated that I had become something more yet less all at the same time. That I had become the girl they all felt like they had to protect.

The girl that was broken.

I didn't want Olly to protect me. I wanted... I don't know. More.

"You okay?" His voice was so low that I knew I was the only one to hear his question, and I knew he was trying to spare me from the others.

"Of course." I laughed and tried to deflect his concern. I splashed water at his chest and shivered. "There was just no way I was letting you throw me in this water."

"It's just..." His gaze ran down my body, and I knew that he was overthinking the way I tensed above him. He overthought everything.

"I'm fine, Olly." I gave him a look that begged him to drop it before running my hand over the water.

He didn't believe me. I could see the doubt staring back at me, and I hated it. I hated how breakable he thought I was. I knew everything that happened with Lucas had affected him as much as it did Beck. They felt betrayed and defensive, but I wished that I could just take it all away.

I never wanted to think about it again.

I never wanted to remember how idiotic I had been with

Lucas. I didn't want to still feel his hands on my skin when I had a night of restless sleep that startled me awake.

But more than any of that, I didn't want Olly to look at me like he was looking at me now. Like I was damaged.

"This water is cold as hell." I startled and looked over at Carson just as he pushed past me into the ocean. His arms wrapped around his chest, and he was tiptoeing through the water with a wince. "I'm pretty sure my dick just shriveled away."

I chuckled and let my shoulders relax as I turned toward him. "Poor Allie."

"He'll come back out to play for her." Carson winked at me, and I rolled my eyes. Allie caught up to him in the water and smacked his arm.

"You are so inappropriate."

"Yeah, but you love that about me." He wrapped his arms around her and pulled her farther into the water with him.

I followed them, step after step, taking me farther away from Olly, but his fingers trailed against mine under the water. My chest fluttered, and I looked back at him over my shoulder. His attention was on Carson, and if I still hadn't felt his skin on mine, I would have thought I was imagining the entire thing.

"Did you get that package from the university yesterday?" Olly asked, and my back straightened.

"Yeah." Carson tucked Allie tighter against his chest, and she smiled up at him as she ran her fingers over his skin. Jealousy bloomed in my chest at what they had. I was so happy for both of them, but I was also envious. "Thank fuck they gave us a place together. I was ready to go kick down Coach's door if they didn't."

"Because he's going to care what the new freshman on

the team want?" Olly cocked an eyebrow and his fingers slipped from mine.

"He will if he wants us to play worth a damn. I'm high maintenance. I need you near or I won't do well." Carson batted his eyelashes at Olly, and I snorted out a laugh even as my chest was tightening.

Olly was leaving.

"Plus, I won't have to put a sock on the door whenever Allie comes to visit. You'll just know."

"Oh my God." Allie slapped him again before pressing her forehead against his chest. "I swear, you're so damn embarrassing."

"If you're embarrassed now, maybe we do need a sock." Carson chuckled and wagged his eyebrows.

"I'll just find someone to stay with whenever Allie visits." Olly shuddered with a laugh. "I don't need to hear all that."

"Oh! Like a girl?" Carson teased him, but it felt like a dagger to my chest.

I swallowed and ran my fingers through the water. Allie looked over at me, and I knew that she could see right through me. It didn't matter how much I had practiced schooling my features when it came to Olly. The pain of imagining him with someone else was a punch to the gut that I couldn't hide.

No amount of preparing myself for the inevitable helped. Not in the slightest. I wasn't foolish enough to think that Olly wasn't going to go to college and be with other girls. I knew that he was probably sleeping with girls here.

Of course, he was.

But he didn't rub it in my face here. I saw the way girls looked at him, the amount of attention he got, and I didn't blame them. Olly was handsome, and he was also different.

He was so damn different than every other guy I had ever met.

He didn't see me because of my money, my family, or my looks. Olly saw the real me that I wasn't sure anyone else ever had. He saw me when no one else seemed to be looking.

He didn't need his dark brown hair, the dark stubble that covered his face, or the golden tan that coated his skin. He would be the most attractive guy in Clermont Bay without all that.

He always had been.

And I was sure that the girls in California would notice it as easily as I did.

"I'd rather sleep in the locker room than listen to you two," Olly joked, and I wondered if he did so for my benefit.

"Where are Beck and Josie?" I shielded my eyes from the blinding sun and looked back up at my house.

"Beck was helping Josie get into her bikini when we came down, so I doubt we'll see them anytime soon." Allie giggled and wrapped her arms around Carson's neck.

Carson nuzzled against her and Allie giggled harder. I felt like I was eavesdropping on a private moment between them, so I quickly turned away and looked back to Olly.

"I think I'm going to get out." I nodded my head toward the beach, but he grabbed my hand under the water again and tugged me toward him.

"I'm going to be gone to California soon. Don't you want to spend all the time with me you can before I leave?" He gave me a teasing smile, and his fingers toyed with mine.

"Please don't remind me." I pouted playfully even though I really didn't want to be reminded of it, and he pushed my hair over my shoulder. He lingered there, his gaze boring into me, and my mouth fell open as I tried to breathe.

His gaze dropped there, watching my mouth for far too long to ever be considered innocent. It lowered further, dragging over every inch of me before he pulled me farther out into the water with my hand in his.

I didn't fight him. I could barely think with the way he was looking at me, and I followed him into the water without another thought about the cold. My breasts sank into the water before it lapped against my collarbones. We were far enough from Allie and Carson now that I could barely hear their murmurs.

"I hate that look on your face." He lifted his free hand and ran it along my jaw. I shivered under his touch, and I felt like I was falling into him. "You can come to visit me all the time with Allie." He was searching my face, but I had no damn clue what he was looking for. Whatever it was, I would gladly give it to him. I would hand over any part of me that he wanted.

"And sleep in the locker room?" I managed to joke, and he laughed softly against me. He was so close that I could feel the slight rumble of his chest against mine.

"I'll get a really good surround sound system to drown them out." His eyes sparkled with mischief. "Then we can just hide out in my room."

It was right on the tip of my tongue to ask him what he'd do with his girlfriend when I came to visit, but I bit it back. Olly wasn't even mine, but I still sounded like a jealous girlfriend who wasn't willing to let him go. Not even a little bit.

"What is it?" He cocked his head to the side as he studied me, and his fingers locked with mine under the water. Always in the shadows.

"Nothing." I shook my head, and I wished with everything inside me that it were the truth.

"Don't lie to me. You know I can read you better than that." His fingers tightened along with my chest.

I wanted to scream. I wanted to do anything that would stop me from feeling like I was going crazy. "Honestly, it's nothing."

"Frankie."

"Olly," I said his name with the same exasperated exhale in which he said mine.

"You know you'll always be my girl even when I'm there." His words sounded so sincere, but I knew that they meant something different to him than they did to me. I was his girl like I was Beck's or Carson's. I was his friend, his little sister, the furthest thing from what I wanted to be.

"Yeah." I nodded and attempted to pull away from him, but he refused to loosen his grip on me.

"What's wrong then?" His gaze fell from my eyes to my mouth, and everything inside me screamed at me to close the gap between us. I desperately wanted to kiss him to see if his lips tasted exactly like I imagined they would.

I wondered if they would be as gentle as his hands were against mine or if he would lose control at the first taste of me. Would the calm, controlled Olly cease to exist or would he remain that disciplined as I fell apart around him?

"I don't think your girlfriends will really like me coming to California to visit you." I was honest with him for the first time in what felt like forever. We never talked about this. We never ventured further than the secret touches and longing moments that I was starting to think were one-sided.

"I don't have any girlfriends, Frankie."

"But you will." I nodded because I knew that was the truth, and I needed the reminder more than he did.

"And you will have guys dying for your attention." A

deep line formed between his brows as they scrunched together, and I could have sworn that look was one of jealousy.

"Oh, yes." I pulled my hand from his and leaned back, letting the cold water soak into my hair. "Because I'm such a hot commodity now."

"I see the way they all look at you." He stared down at me for a second before his gaze roamed down my body. It was as if he was physically touching me. Everywhere his gaze went, a trail of electricity followed. "They all want you, Frankie."

"Not all of them." My stomach tightened, and his gaze stopped there. His brow was still scrunched as if he was trying to work something out in his head, and I was dying to reach up and smooth it out.

"All of them. Trust me."

I stood back up, digging my toes into the sand, and watched as he clenched his hands into fists at his sides.

"Even you?" I whispered the question, and for a second, I didn't think he heard me. He was so fucking still that I couldn't breathe, and I wished I could take back what I had asked him.

"You know I can't answer that."

"Why not?" I could feel the rivulets of water running down my body from my hair, and his gaze followed their path.

"It's not fair to either of us." He finally looked at me, really looked at me, and I hated what I saw.

"Because of my brother?" I was as frustrated as I sounded.

"Because of him. Because of..." He trailed off, so I finished the sentence for him so he didn't have to say it.

"Lucas?" I crossed my arms over my chest, but it wasn't

enough. I felt so exposed even saying his name. "What he did has nothing to do with you and me."

But when I thought about it, all I could think about were the things Olly had said to me before. If only I had listened to him. If only I had realized how much better Olly was then, then maybe...

"I know that." He ran his wet hand through his hair, and his jaw clenched. I didn't know if it was frustration or anger, but I didn't deserve either. "That's not what I meant. It's just that he made things harder. Beck would never forgive me."

I knew what he was saying was true, but I still hated it. I wasn't just his best friend's little sister. I was his best friend's little sister who was assaulted by her brother's other best friend. By a guy I had once trusted as much as the rest of them.

As much as I did him.

But his words still cut through me and ripped open wounds I tried not to think about.

"And I'm leaving. This is my last summer before—"

"I know," I interrupted him. My head was starting to throb from my deep, rapid pulse that coursed through me. "Before this is all over."

I planted a fake smile on my face and looked up at him. *Hide it, Frankie. Don't let him see how badly this hurts you.*

"That doesn't mean..." He stepped closer to me, and I wasn't sure if he even realized he was doing it.

"Mean what?" I asked, and I was so damn desperate for his answer.

"That..." He hesitated again, and I wanted to shake him.

"Just say it, Olly. Say what you're really thinking." My heart hammered, and no matter how hard I tried, I couldn't calm it down.

"That I want you any less." His gaze was molten as it met mine. "I can be halfway across the world from you, and I'll still want you more than you'll ever realize."

I tried to swallow down a breath, but it felt impossible.

"Olly," I whispered his name, and it sounded like a plea.

We were so close now that I could feel the heat of his skin. He reached for my hand again, but the moment his skin met mine, I heard my brother's voice behind us.

"How cold is it?" Beck called out, and Olly dropped his hand from mine so quickly you would think I burned him.

"Freezing." Olly laughed as he took a step back from me and ran his fingers down his neck. I wrapped my arms around my chest as I watched him.

Olly stared up at my brother and didn't meet my eyes.

Pain sliced through my chest because I wanted him to pick me. I knew that was selfish. I knew that I shouldn't have wished for something that would eventually hurt someone that I loved, but I did.

Despite what Beck thought or wanted, hell, what anyone thought, I wanted Olly.

I wanted him to choose me and to make this constant buzzing in my head disappear. More than anything, I wanted him to choose me in a way that made me feel like I wasn't their burden.

I was tired of being the girl who didn't have more because of what happened to her. I was exhausted of being the girl who couldn't want to be with someone because I should have been frightened by anything sexual.

I wasn't scared of anything when it came to Olly except for the fact that he may not have wanted me the way I wanted him.

That thought terrified me.

He finally glanced back in my direction, and the way he was looking at me now was so different than only moments before. "This can't happen, Frankie." His hand motioned gently between the two of us. "I'm not good for you. You need to live. Have fun. This is your senior year, and you don't need to spend it stuck with me."

Anger bubbled to the surface, but I tried to push it down. Even though I tried not to be, I was angry with him for a choice he was making for me even though it was the last thing I wanted.

But anger felt so much better than desperation.

CHAPTER 2

OLLY

I pushed through the crowd in search of Frankie. She had barely spoken to me since yesterday, and I wasn't dumb enough to pretend like I didn't know why.

I should have never opened my fucking mouth.

I had made it this long keeping myself in check, and trust me, I had wanted to tell Frankie everything for as long as I could remember. I wanted to whisper every single thing I was thinking about her against her skin while I explored every inch of her perfect body. I was dying to taste her lips, to taste her moans.

I was desperate to just hold her and make her feel like more than anyone had ever made her feel before.

Maybe one day. That thought echoed in my mind on repeat, and I tried to quiet it. I was meant to be the guy Frankie needed and not the guy I wanted to be to her. One day meant someone would get hurt. One day meant that I was going to have to face everything I felt for her, and I didn't know if I dared.

I knew how big of a coward that made me.

Because even though she looked at me like she lost as much sleep over me as I did her, I was fucking terrified that she didn't.

I was frozen by the thought of not being able to breathe while I was simply someone who had been helping her survive through her pain.

It was so much easier to not say anything at all than to face that.

I needed her, and she needed so much more. Everything I felt for her felt chaotic and reckless, and fuck, that felt so dangerous.

Because regardless of what she wanted, we couldn't have any of it.

Beck would never forgive me if I crossed that line with her. He may have before. Before Lucas fucked everything up, but he trusted me. He trusted me and Carson to protect his sister just like he would.

He had trusted Lucas that way once upon a time too, and he fucking broke him when he betrayed him. He changed Beck in a way that I couldn't describe, and I knew there was no going back from that.

But none of that compared to what he did to Frankie.

Every time I thought about it, I wanted to kill him. He was just allowed to walk around, to live, after what he did, and my hands shook with fury every time I saw him.

I was meant to be another one of her protectors, not the guy fantasizing about her like I was an addict and she had become my drug of choice.

But fuck, she was an addiction that I wasn't sure I could break.

But I knew that she was the one capable of breaking me. I had become a safe place for Frankie, a shield against the rest of the world, and more than anything, I feared that safety was where her desire lied. While I was utterly consumed by her, I had become her harbor.

I spotted her standing next to a group of people I knew from school, and she was laughing at something the guy next to her had just said. I watched as she backed away from him less than half a step as he leaned closer to her. He didn't have a clue. There were some things that she always did to protect herself, and they were almost undetectable if you weren't looking.

But I always saw.

"Hey." I stepped up next to her and pressed my hand to the small of her back. Her body sagged against my hand just the tiniest bit as if it recognized the feel of me before she turned in my direction. I could physically feel the tension leaving her body, and I instantly went on alert.

Had someone made her feel uncomfortable or was she just overwhelmed altogether?

"Hi." She barely met my eyes as she spoke, and I knew that I had really fucked things up when she turned back to the guy in front of her and gave him her attention.

I recognized him, but I couldn't remember his damn name. John? Jimmy? Fuck, what was it?

"Hey, man." I nodded to him and tightened my grip on Frankie. My fingers bunched in her shirt, and I knew there was no way she didn't notice. "I'm Olly."

"Of course." He chuckled and looked back and forth between me and my girl. "I'm Jarod."

Jarod. Shit, I knew that.

"Jarod, do you mind if I borrow Frankie for just a second? We really need to talk."

He opened his mouth to answer, but Frankie beat him to

it. "Actually, it'll have to wait." She looked back at me and gave me a look that told me she wasn't fucking around. There was so much fire in her gaze that it almost hid the sadness that was always lingering. "Jarod was just about to show me something."

I tightened my grip on the back of her shirt but smiled. "Okay. I can wait."

I wasn't sure if I would ever stop waiting.

She didn't answer me, and I didn't hang around to see what the hell Jarod was going to show her. Frankie rarely ever talked to guys at a party; most of the time she was by my side if she even came at all, but I knew that this probably had everything to do with what I said yesterday.

I grabbed a beer out of a cooler as I passed by and clenched my hand around the cold glass as I walked away from her and out the back of the house.

I spotted Carson as soon as I walked out the door, and he cocked his head to the side as if he was studying me. I wondered if he had been watching me with her the whole time.

Fuck. I needed to stop being an idiot. If Carson could see through me so easily, then that meant other people could too.

"What's up?" I twisted the top off my beer and brought it to my lips without waiting for anyone's reply. Josie was sitting on Beck's lap and leaning against his chest. Allie was standing behind Carson with her arms wrapped around his stomach.

My chest tightened as I looked over at them all. I was happy for all of them. More than happy, but I wanted that. I wanted to be able to pull Frankie out here and hold her the way they were holding them.

But more than anything, I just wanted to pull her away from that douchebag in there.

I looked back through the door, and my gaze met hers before she quickly looked away. She smiled at something he said, but her arms were crossed over her chest. She didn't look at him for long. Her eyes bounced around the room and watched those around her. She was always so aware of her surroundings, and my stomach knotted because I hated the thought that she always felt she needed to.

Jarod was smiling at her like he was the luckiest guy alive, and I knew he wasn't picking up on one bit of her unease.

And even though I wanted to hate him, I knew that wasn't his fault.

Frankie was gorgeous. Her dark brown hair and tanned skin were a lethal combination, and she had become so good at hiding her mistrust.

Frankie was capable of making you forget anything other than her even existed.

She looked back up at him, and I knew if he wasn't distracted by her perfect pink lips, then he was looking into her eyes. They were so dark brown that they were almost black, and she showed so much emotion with them. I had never met anyone who could be so vulnerable with just a single look.

But she was.

With me, she never seemed to hide it.

It was something that I both loved and hated about her.

I almost always knew how she felt, but that meant I could never hide from it either. Whenever I was doing my fucking best to bury everything I was feeling for her, she simply looked up at me and all the work I had done was unraveled.

"Where's Frankie?" Beck looked up at me like I should have the answer. "She came with us, but I haven't seen her in a while." He stood like he was going to go look for her, but I quickly nodded into the house.

"In there." I didn't pretend like I had taken my eyes off her for a single second and pointed to where she stood with the neck of my beer bottle. "She told me that Jarod was showing her something."

"What the fuck is he showing her?" Beck growled, and I wished that he would storm in there and pull her away from him. But that didn't happen.

"Leave her alone." Josie gripped his jaw in her hand and turned his gaze back to meet hers. "You all are going to have to let the girl live a little whether you like it or not."

"Not with Jarod," Beck grumbled, and Carson snorted out a laugh. But I had to agree with Beck on this one.

"Yes. With Jarod." Josie sounded so irritated. "Or Tom or Billy or Enrique. It's not up to the three of you who Frankie decides to date, and pretty soon, the three of you will have graduated and she's going to get all the attention they've been too scared to give her."

She was right, but she was also wrong. It wasn't up to us who Frankie decided to date, but I would be damned if I let my girl fall for some fucking douchebag. She had already been hurt so much in her lifetime, and she didn't deserve any more. Not from them and not from me.

Frankie deserved to experience life and have fun. She deserved so much more than anyone in this town had ever given her, and I hated the idea of her getting stuck.

Beck said something back to Josie, but I was too busy

watching Frankie to hear what he said. Jarod moved closer to her and pressed his hand against the small of her back, my spot, and his hand laid flat against her skin where her shirt had lifted. I watched her tense under his touch, but she didn't move away. I downed the rest of my beer as my blood raced through my veins.

I think Beck was asking a question, maybe to me, maybe to someone else, but I didn't care either way. I tossed my beer bottle in the trash before pushing back through the door and making my way toward Frankie.

She smiled up at Jarod, but her jaw was clenched tightly. Why the fuck was she letting him touch her?

Her gaze lifted to me, and I saw the small flash of relief in her eyes even though she tried to hide it.

"Frankie, I need to talk to you for a sec." I crossed my arms and stared down at where Jarod was still touching her. I was seconds away from ripping his damn arm off.

"Seriously, Olly?" She sighed my name, and Jarod slowly pulled his hand off her back.

I finally looked back up at her and the relief I had seen a few moments before was gone and had been replaced with irritation. Good. I was beyond irritated myself.

"You don't have to talk to me if you don't want. I can let Beck come in here like he wanted to." I hiked my thumb over my shoulder to where I knew her brother was still sitting. No doubt they were all watching us, but I couldn't bring myself to care.

"Fine." She practically growled and pulled away from him. "Jarod, excuse me. I'll be right back."

She stomped away a few steps without waiting for me, and I took a step closer to Jarod. For all I knew, he was a great guy. Hell, he could probably treat Frankie far better than I would ever get the opportunity to, but I wasn't willing to give him the opportunity either. Seeing his hand on her felt like he was violating something that didn't belong to him.

He wasn't right for her.

"She won't be back."

His gaze flew up to mine, and I was glad I had his attention.

"I thought Frankie was single."

"She's not." I shook my head as I clenched my jaw, and even though it was a lie, it felt like the most honest thing I had said all day. "So I suggest you stay away from her."

I walked past him in search of Frankie, and I didn't have to go far. She was still only a few steps away, and she was staring at me like she wanted to murder me. I knew that she had heard everything I just said, but I couldn't bring myself to be sorry. I meant it whether it was right or wrong.

She stormed away from me as I headed toward her, and I couldn't blame her for being pissed. But she had to know there was no way in hell I could just sit back and watch her with someone else. It wasn't fair. I was more than aware of that.

Hurting her was the last thing I wanted to do, but I didn't know how to love her and not hurt her in some way.

I didn't know how to be this guy who had become her protector while also not making her feel stuck.

Frankie had watched me with other girls, and there had been plenty. But I hadn't touched anyone else in over two years. Two fucking excruciating years.

I tried. Trust me, I wished that I could just fuck someone else and get Frankie out of my system, but it didn't work that way. She was embedded so deeply in me that I wasn't sure I would ever be able to get her out. I wasn't sure that I wanted to.

I snatched her hand in mine as I caught up to her, but she jerked it away as she kept walking.

"Frankie," I sighed, and she only stormed faster down the hallway. "Hold on. Just fucking talk to me."

She stopped in her tracks, my chest almost hitting her back, and she spun toward me. There was so much fire in her eyes as she stared up at me. "Why the hell would you tell him that I'm with someone." She held out her hands to her sides as her voice rose. "I think it's clear as fucking day that I'm not."

A few people turned in our direction before I gripped her wrist in my hand and tugged her farther down the hall. The first door I tried to open was locked, and I cursed under my breath as I went for the next. Thankfully, this one opened, and I pulled Frankie inside behind me before closing the door.

"Will you calm down?"

"No!" She jerked her wrist out of my touch and pressed her trembling hands into her hips. "I will not calm down, Olly. I don't know who the hell you think you are, but you do not get to decide who I do or don't date."

I took a step toward her, and she held up her hand to keep me at bay. "You don't get to decide who I kiss or touch or fuck." Her voice shook on the last word, and I pressed my chest against her hand dend closed the space between us whether she wanted me to or not.

"You know that's a lie." I stared down at her and moved some of her dark brown hair out of her face. The room was dark with only the light of the moon filtering in through the window, but I could still see her. I had always been able to see her.

"It's not." She shook her head before I pressed my hand against her neck and stopped her movement with my thumb.

I felt the way her breath trembled in and out of her throat under my touch. She was so fucking beautiful. Far too beautiful for anyone at this damn party, but I couldn't stop myself from touching her. I lifted my thumb and ran it across her full bottom lip, and it was so damn soft. Softer than I had ever imagined.

"You and I both know it is." I pushed even closer to her, and her hand flattened between us. "I'd kill that asshole before I let him have what is mine."

She let out a whimper that almost dropped me to my knees. "I'm not yours, Olly." Her words were no longer sure, the bite from earlier had all but disappeared.

"You are." I leaned in and ran my nose along her jaw. "It doesn't matter what anyone else says or thinks. You are mine."

She shoved against my chest, but I didn't budge. I couldn't. Not when I was so fucking close to her, and I could smell the slightest hint of coconut on her skin.

"Olly," she whispered my name, and it sounded like the sweetest plea on her lips.

I couldn't control myself. After all this time, I couldn't wait another second. I lifted her chin until she was forced to look back up at me, and I closed the gap between us. Without even truly deciding to, my mouth met hers in a rush. She moaned into my mouth as she met my lips with just as much force.

I ran my tongue over the seam of her lips, and she

opened without hesitation. My body felt like it was on fire as her tongue ran over mine. I kissed her like I may never get the chance again, and I could feel myself losing bits of who I was in her with every passing second.

Frankie pulled her arms from between us before she wrapped them around my shoulders. Her fingers tangled in the back of my hair, and there was the slightest sting of pain as she forced me impossibly closer to her.

What started as a rushed, frantic kiss became slower and more purposeful. Frankie wrapped one of her legs around my waist, and I pressed firmly against her. She didn't stop me. Instead, she met my hips with her own, and when I gripped her ass in my hands she lifted her other leg and wrapped fully around me. She began to move, her hips as slow as her tongue, and I thought I was going to die from the torture.

I felt so impatient for her touch. I wanted to feel her everywhere. I wanted to sink into the wildest parts of her.

I ran my tongue and lips over her jaw and down her neck, and she tasted exactly as she smelled. Frankie was a mixture of sunshine and the ocean. She was like that exact spot where they met, where everything seemed magical, elusive, and so far out of reach.

"Olly, please," she whispered my name, and it sounded like a fucking prayer.

She was still rolling her hips against mine, and I knew she could feel how hard I was for her. I could feel her too. Every inch of her moved against me in a way that should have had me questioning her innocence, and I moved a hand from her ass to slowly creep up her body. Her stomach tremored beneath my touch as my fingers ran over her skin, but there wasn't an ounce of fear in her eyes. It was one hundred percent raw anticipation that was waiting for me.

Frankie wanted me. I was absolutely certain that she wanted me physically, and God, I wanted her too. I had wanted her for so long that this moment felt like a recurrent dream that had haunted me night after night.

Every time I closed my eyes, she was the only thing I could picture.

She was both hedonic and torturous at the same time.

And here she was beneath my touch and still, she felt so far out of reach. I cupped her small breast in my hand, and I watched as I slowly dragged my thumb over her nipple. She was still fully clothed, but the fabric did little to hide what lay beneath. She moaned loudly, and for the first time since we had walked in the room, my gaze flew to the door behind her that anyone could easily walk in through.

What the fuck were we doing?

I kissed her again because there was no way I could stop. I drank in the taste of her, the feel of her, and she held me to her as she intensified her movements against me as I bit down on her bottom lip before soothing the pain with my tongue. Frankie's hips surged forward as if she couldn't control the movement, and I could only imagine how wet her pussy was.

I was dying to know. I was dying to rip her pants down her legs and bury my face in her sweet pussy until everyone in this entire fucking place knew who she belonged to.

I gripped her ass in my hands again and took a steadying breath against her mouth. There is no way that she would stop this. She didn't give a shit about what her brother or anyone else thought, but I did. Beck was not just my best friend. He was my brother, and he would hate me for this.

This wasn't a normal brother's best friend situation. He entrusted me to protect her, to be the opposite of Lucas, and I was betraying his trust with every second that passed.

But more importantly, I felt like I was betraying hers. She felt safe with me, and I didn't want to take advantage of that feeling.

"Frankie," I breathed her name against her lips and tried to force her hips from mine. She tightened her legs against my waist and her arms on my shoulders.

"Don't." She shook her head, and there was a flash of regret in her eyes. She knew what I was doing. She knew that I couldn't go any further than this. That I had already done too much.

"We can't do this." I searched her eyes before she looked away from me and dropped her feet back to the ground. I would've done anything to take that look away from her at that moment, but I didn't know how. I didn't know how to navigate this without hurting her or fucking up my friendship with Beck.

After everything Frankie had been through, here I was being a damn idiot at another party, taking advantage of her body. She deserved better than this. She deserved more than I would ever be able to give her. But fuck, I wanted to be the one to figure it out.

"It's fine." Frankie straightened her shirt and tucked her hair behind her ears. She still refused to look at me, and her chest still heaved in her attempts to catch her breath.

"Frankie." I reached out for her, but she slipped away from my touch before I could touch her.

"No." She shook her head, and I could see the hurt all over her face. Her chin trembled as her next words hit me. "You don't get to do that. You don't get to pretend like you want me when no one else is around. I'm so tired of being in the shadows."

She was right, and I had no idea what I should say to make any of this up to her. I was desperate to take back what I had done even though I knew I would truly never regret a single second of it. Even if I knew that I should.

She didn't give me the opportunity to do anything. She opened the door before I could string together a few words to tell her how I was feeling, and she stopped dead in her tracks when she saw Beck standing on the other side of the door.

"There you are." He grabbed her hand in his and pulled her toward him, and it took him a few seconds before he finally noticed me behind her. "What the fuck were you two doing?" He narrowed his eyes as he looked back and forth between us.

My heart hammered in my chest because a part of me wanted to just tell him the truth. I wanted to tell him that I had been in love with his sister for a long time, that the things we had done behind that door were something neither one of us could control, but I knew he wouldn't understand that. Beck was my best friend, but he was also irrational and hotheaded, and rightfully so. He was overprotective of Frankie, we all were, but he had reason to be. I couldn't be angry at him for it.

He felt like he failed to protect her once, and he refused to do so again.

"What does it matter?" Frankie huffed and crossed her arms. "What I do with anyone isn't up to you all."

"Frankie," Beck said her name with an exasperated tone. This is a conversation, or better yet, argument, that they had at least a hundred times before.

"What if I told you that I just fucked Olly in that room?" Beck stiffened at her question, and my gaze snapped to her. "What the hell would you do about it if that were the case?"

Beck looked back and forth between me and Frankie, and I couldn't fucking breathe. Because even though we did cross the line in that room, it wasn't what she was saying, and I knew she was just trying to get a rise out of her brother. More than that, she was trying to get a rise out of me.

"I'd kill him." Beck didn't hesitate with his answer, and even though I already knew it, my stomach dropped at his confession.

"Whatever." Frankie rolled her eyes and laughed at her brother. "He's your best friend."

"You're right." He nodded and his gaze landed on me. So much passed between us with that one look than he would ever say out loud. "Which means I trust him more than anyone else. He would never betray me like that."

"Being with me is not a betrayal," Frankie practically screamed, and I stepped forward before this went any further.

"For me, it is." Beck looked back at his sister.

"I was just telling her to stay away from Jarod." The lie fell smoothly from my lips, and my chest fucking ached at how easy it was. "I didn't want to see the poor guy get his ass kicked tonight."

Beck grinned, and I knew he was probably picturing it. "Yeah. He's an asshole, Frankie."

"I hate you."

I thought Frankie was talking to her brother, but when I looked up at her, her gaze was directly on me.

CHAPTER 3
FRANKIE

I couldn't look away from Olly long enough to even see my brother. How he could just stand there like nothing had just happened between us was beyond me. I felt like I was going to explode, like every part of me was shaking with the need to touch him, to kiss him, or to slap him across the face.

Olly wanted me as much as I wanted him, but while I made a conscious decision to want him, his want had been nothing more than a slip of his better judgment.

He regretted everything we had just done even though it had been the best kiss of my life. I knew how sad that was. I knew that Olly was far more experienced than I was, and this was probably just another kiss from any other girl to him. But it meant something to me.

It meant more.

"You'll get over it." Beck laughed because he thought I was talking to him, but I wasn't. I had meant what I said when I told Olly I hated him. At that moment, I did hate him for choosing Beck over me, for letting his friendship with my brother dictate how far we took things, but at the same time, I knew that I could never hate him.

Not really.

"I'm going back out to the party." I pointed down the hall where the loud music was still playing. "And I'm going to find a guy to kiss who doesn't look at me like I'm the biggest mistake of his life." I stared straight at Olly with a heaviness in my chest that I couldn't shake, and I didn't care what Beck thought about what I just said.

"Frankie." Olly looked frantic as he searched my eyes, and I watched his hand unclench at his side to reach out for me. But I refused to let him touch me again. I was too damn angry.

I walked past him before he was able to get to me, and I didn't stop when I heard him or Beck call out my name. I kept pushing through the party, moving past the crowd of people. I spotted Jarod still in the kitchen, but when my gaze met his, he quickly looked away. That was fucking fine with me. I wasn't really interested in him anyway, and no guy that could be so easily intimidated by Olly was worth the effort.

It was better to figure that out early. Even if I had only been talking to him because I desperately wanted to get a reaction out of Olly.

I pushed through the kitchen and made my way out to the back porch. I was met by Josie and Allie staring at me with concerned looks on their faces as soon as the warm air kissed my skin. Allie moved out of Carson's touch, and they both came straight for me before I could say a word.

"Do you want to head home?" Josie asked as soon as she reached me, and I knew that she would leave my asshole brother here and take me home if that was what I wanted. But it wasn't.

I didn't want to go home and wallow in my own fucking pity. I had done that far too much, and I promised myself I wouldn't do it again. Not over some boy.

Even if it was him.

"No." I shook my head. "Let's do something fun."

"What do you want to do?" Allie smiled at me, but there was so much hesitation in that one look. "We're at a party."

I shook my head as a thought about what I wanted, but it wasn't something that the three of us could discuss right now. "I want to get a drink."

They looked at each other with a look of concern, and I knew they thought it was a bad idea. But I didn't care. Everything I did lately seemed like a bad idea.

And I never drank. Not anymore. Not since everything happened with Lucas, but right now, I felt powerless. I felt like every small decision in my life was being made by someone else, and I hated it.

I just wanted to do whatever I wanted. Whether it was smart or not, didn't matter.

I couldn't have Olly because of Lucas and Beck, and the stupid fucking notion that I was somehow everyone else's responsibility. I didn't want to be their burden.

I had become their obligation, and my chest ached at the thought of them seeing me like that.

And I was so tired of making decisions based on what happened in the past. I didn't want to make choices out of fear.

"Okay." Josie nodded. "How about we all get one drink?"

"That's a start." I shrugged as I drew in a deep breath then released it, and she laughed as we made our way over to the keg. I didn't recognize the guy pouring beers, but I didn't give him much thought either. I was too busy chewing on my thumbnail and watching the back door as Olly and Beck pushed through it.

Olly's gaze met mine as soon as he stepped through the threshold, and I jerked my gaze back to the keg.

I knew that I didn't stand a chance in hiding how much he affected me, but I refused to fall at his feet and beg him to give me more than he was willing to give. If he wanted to be just friends, then fine. I could do that.

I would force myself to forget about what it had just felt like to have his mouth and hands on me. I would bury the feeling of being at home in his touch in the very back of my mind.

But I couldn't force myself to unlove him, and I honestly didn't want to.

"Thank you." I took the beer from the guy at the keg, and he smiled up at me with the softest smile.

"Of course, beautiful."

I tightened my hand around my cup and tried to swallow past the heaviness in my throat as I smiled back at him. I should have felt something at hearing him call me beautiful, but I didn't feel anything. Not when I took in his handsome smile or the way he was looking at me like he would have given the world to take me into that room Olly had just forced me out of.

I searched his face and took in his unruly blond hair, but the only thought that crossed my mind was that he wasn't Olly.

I turned away from him and followed Allie back to where the boys were standing. Olly was still watching me. I didn't need to look up at him to know that. I lifted the beer to my mouth and didn't stop when the cold alcohol tasted so bitter on my tongue. I drank more than I knew I should, but deep down, I knew that none of them would let anything happen to me.

Not again.

"Whoa, Frankie." Beck looked concerned as he looked back and forth between me and my drink, but I didn't care. Not tonight.

I didn't reply to his comment. Instead, I swirled the beer in my cup before bringing it back to my mouth and finishing the cup. When I looked up at my friends, all I could see was concern staring back at me from all of them.

From everyone except Olly because I didn't dare look at him.

"I'm going to get another." I shook my empty cup in my hand and pressed my lips together.

"I think you've had enough." Beck's voice was firm, but it was muddled by Olly's. "I'll go with you."

"Nope." I pointed back and forth between both of them and let out a laugh that didn't have an ounce of humor. "I don't need babysitters tonight. You two go find someone else to ruin their night."

I turned away from them before either of them could answer, and headed back to the keg. My stomach tightened as I walked away from them, but I begged it to stop. I just didn't want to feel any of these damn feelings for just a little while.

"That was quick." Keg guy smiled at me before taking the cup from my hand. He was teasing, but he wasn't reprimanding me, and it felt nice.

I shook out my arms and tried to release some of the tension that was trapped inside of me. "I needed a drink."

"Boyfriend problems?" He cocked his head to the side,

and his blond hair flopped into his forehead a little. He was cute. Cuter than I had originally given him credit for.

"More like asshole problems."

He chuckled at my answer and started refilling my cup.

"What about you?" I looked around him. He was basically out here all by himself except for the people who were stopping by for more alcohol. "How did you get stuck manning the keg?"

"Ah. It's not too bad." He handed me my drink before pushing his hair back out of his face. "All the pretty girls come out here for a drink."

I could feel heat rising in my cheeks, and I wondered if he always wore that easy smile on his face. I didn't even know him, but it felt like it fit him so perfectly.

"So, you've met a lot of pretty girls tonight?"

His smile widened as he chuckled softly, and I had a feeling that this guy was genuine. "None as pretty as you."

"If I hadn't just chugged my beer, I'd call you on that lie, but I'll let it slide." I took another sip of my beer as he ran his hand over his jaw before pushing it out in my direction.

"I'm Harry."

"Frankie." I slid my hand in his and let him shake it. It was just another hand that made me feel nothing from its touch.

"Do you go to Clermont High?" He looked me over as if he was trying to place if he had met me before. "I swear I would know you if you do."

"No." I tucked my hair behind my ear as I felt a bit of tension ease from my stomach. "I go to Prep."

"Ahhh. A Prep girl, huh?"

I looked him over from head to toe and didn't answer his question. "A High boy, huh?"

"That's fair." He chuckled, and I genuinely liked the sound.

The fact that he didn't know me was a blessing. It meant he didn't know who my family was, who my brother was, or what had happened to me. Those three things were all most people knew about me these days.

"Can I get a beer?" I heard Olly's voice, but I didn't turn to look at him. My spine straightened as I stared straight ahead at Harry.

"So, Harry, do you have a girlfriend?" I tucked my hand in my back pocket to keep it from shaking.

He looked up from where he was pouring Olly's drink, and there was a spark of surprise in his eyes. "I don't." He looked back and forth between me and Olly quickly.

I nodded my head as I tried to work up my courage. I could feel the anger rolling off Olly next to me, and somehow that only seemed to fuel me on. He didn't have the right to be angry. "I'd love to go out with you sometime if you're interested."

"Absolutely." He over-poured Olly's beer and spilled some over on his hand. He chuckled before shaking the liquid off his hand and holding out Olly's drink for him. He quickly pulled his phone out of his pocket and handed it out to me without another glance in Olly's direction.

"Give me your number, and we can nail down the details."

"Perfect." I glanced up at Olly who was openly glaring at me. Even he couldn't hide the anger that was staring back down at me, and I let my gaze travel down to his flattened lips. "Can you hold this?" I held out my beer in his direction, and it took him a few seconds before he reached out and took it. His fingers trailed over mine, and I knew it wasn't an accident.

Olly didn't know what the hell he wanted from me, but I was sure that he didn't want anyone else to have me. He was unnerving me, trying to distract me from the boy in front of me, but I refused to allow him.

I gripped Harry's phone in both hands as I entered my number with trembling fingers.

"Here you go." I handed it back to him as he grinned.

"I'll text you." He slid his phone into his pocket before his eyes finally went back to Olly. I knew he could feel the tension between us. It would have been impossible for him not to.

"I look forward to it." I grabbed my beer back from Olly's hand and tried not to react when his fingers met mine again. But the small amount of alcohol I had was already starting to mess with my head, and I was physically incapable of not reacting to him when I was completely sober.

I pushed past him before he could say anything to ruin this moment and headed back in the direction of our friends. I could feel Olly on my heels the entire way, and I became so irrationally angry that he wouldn't leave me alone.

"Can I help you with something?" I spun on my heel until I was facing him. He was so damn close to me, and he didn't dare take a step back to give me any room.

"We need to talk." He was so damn calm as he said it, and it just pissed me off more.

"Oh, no!" I pointed my finger into his chest and ground my teeth. "That ship has sailed, buddy."

"Buddy?" His lips tugged up at the edge into a smile and my back straightened. "Am I your buddy now?"

"I wasn't sure if you wouldn't have preferred for me to call you an asshole." I lifted my beer and took a deep swallow. His brows drew together as he watched me.

"You shouldn't be drinking like that."

"And you shouldn't be telling me what to do."

He stared at me like he wanted to argue, but he didn't. He bit his tongue and watched me, and I desperately wished he would just lean down and kiss me in front of everyone. I leaned closer to him, almost subconsciously, and I couldn't read the look on his face.

"Are you going to go out with Harry?"

I smiled at the fact that he knew his name even though I was sure he was going to ruin it for me. "I am. Why? Do you have a problem with that?"

He worked his jaw as he looked away from me, and I knew he was thinking something he wasn't willing to say. "No." He shook his head. "He seems like a good enough guy."

His words shocked me, and my gaze flew up to meet his. "So you're okay with me kissing him?"

When he didn't answer, I stepped even closer and pressed my hand to his chest. "What if we decide to go further? What if I let him touch me?"

"Frankie." My name was a growl on his lips, and I had to press my thighs together to stop the ache that began there.

"Do you think he would touch me like you did in that room?" I nodded my head toward the house and the smell of his cologne surrounded me. I didn't know if it was that or the alcohol that was making me feel so lightheaded. I really hadn't had that much to drink. "Do you think I will go home at the end of the night and replace your name with his when I touch myself?"

"Fuck," he cursed and gripped my bicep in his hand as if he feared I might slip away. There was a bite of pain in his touch, but I didn't want it to stop. "You've had too much to drink."

"Maybe." I shrugged my shoulders. In reality, I had, but these were things I had wanted to say to him for far too long. I just never had the courage. I had always worried too much about what he would think, but I couldn't bring myself to care tonight. "Or maybe Harry just has me really turned on."

"Stop." It was a command.

"Make me." I was so close to him now that I could lean forward and kiss him if I wanted to. He would stop me, of course, but part of me felt like making him. I wanted him to deny me, to break me even further, because maybe then I could forget about him for just a damn second.

"Everyone is watching us," he whispered, and the sound skated down my spine like fingers.

"I don't care."

"Yes. You do." He nodded and pulled me into his body until I was forced to wrap my arms around him. He hugged me against him like he was as desperate to touch me as I was him, and the smallest moan left my lips at the feel of him. "I'm going home. Let me take you back to your house."

"No." I shook my head and pushed against his chest to step back. "I'm staying."

I didn't want to leave. I refused to just let him take me home and pretend like tonight never happened.

He searched my eyes as he pushed his dark hair out of his face, then he let out a heavy sigh. "Then I guess I'm staying too."

CHAPTER 4

OLLY

Frankie had too much to drink.

And even though I probably should have stopped her, I couldn't bring myself to do it.

She was sitting on top of the patio table, and her head was thrown back in laughter. She was so damn beautiful, especially like this, when there wasn't a single worry on her face.

It felt like it had been forever since I had seen her so carefree.

Beck looked up at his sister and chuckled as he watched her. "Are you about ready to go, wild one? Josie has work tomorrow."

"Nope." Her answer was instant and she dramatically popped the P before she reached out and patted her brother on top of his head. "You all can go ahead, though."

"I'm not leaving you here alone." Beck ran his hand over the back of his neck.

"I'm not alone." She glanced around and her eyes connected with mine for what felt like the first time in hours.

"All of my other bodyguards are here, and I'm certain they won't let me get a hair out of place."

"This is true." Carson chuckled and adjusted Allie on his lap. She was so relaxed against him, but her gaze was still on her friend. "I won't let this little one out of my sight."

"Don't call me that," Frankie huffed and crossed her arms, and I smiled at her reaction. She may not have any worries tonight, but she was still as sassy as ever. Maybe even more so.

"Fine." Beck stood and gripped Josie's hand in his. "We'll see you guys tomorrow." Beck looked back and forth between Carson and me as Josie hugged his sister, and we both knew what that one simple look meant.

It was something that I didn't need to forget.

"I love you, Frankie." He tousled her hair, and she rolled her eyes.

"Love you too."

As soon as Beck pushed through the back door, Frankie clapped her hands and grinned. "It's time for another drink."

"How about we slow down?" I took the seat next to her that Beck had just vacated and I instantly felt more at ease being so close to her.

"How about you kiss my ass, Olly? I am not drunk." She smiled sweetly at me.

"Oh shit." Carson laughed and ran his hand over his mouth, and I wanted to kill him. "I think she might have actually had too much to drink."

"I'm having fun." She swung her legs back and forth at the edge of the table and shrugged. "You all are the party poopers."

"Leave her alone." Allie grinned up at her friend. "She's fine."

"Exactly." Frankie turned toward me with a lazy smile and rested her foot on my thigh. "I'm fine."

"Uh-huh." I gripped her ankle in my hand when she tried to turn away from me, and she paused. "Do you want me to get you another drink then?"

"Please." Her legs widened in front of me, and God, what I wouldn't give for us to be anywhere else. For the two of us to be anyone other than who we were.

"I can do that." Carson and Allie were sitting on the opposite side of the table, and I knew if they wanted to, they could see exactly what I was doing. But I still rubbed my thumb along her ankle as I stared up at her. "Is there anything else I can get you?"

"There are several things." She leaned forward so only I could hear her. "But I don't think you want to hear any of those."

My gaze flew up to meet Carson's, but he quickly looked away and tucked his head against Allie as he spoke to her.

"I don't think you have any idea what I want."

Frankie leaned back again and tapped her finger against her chin. "You know what. I don't." Her foot moved the slightest bit higher on my thigh. "And whose fault is that?"

"Mine."

"Yours." She nodded her head in agreement. "Honestly, a lot of things are your fault."

She lifted her other foot and brought it down to rest on my other knee before leaning forward and resting her elbows on her own.

She looked so damn perfect.

"Do tell." I pressed my fingers into her other ankle. "What am I at fault for now?"

"Everything." She sighed before swallowing harshly and

blinking down at me. "You're too damn handsome for your own good."

I leaned forward until my chest pressed against her shins. "Thank you, but I don't see how that makes me guilty of anything."

"It makes you guilty of a lot of things." She held up her hand and started ticking off fingers as she went. "One, I think about you way too often. Two, no other guy will ask me out because you're always around and you're so pretty that you intimidate them."

"What about Harry?" I looked toward the keg, but Harry had disappeared a while ago.

"And three, I can't get off without thinking about your stupid face."

I heard Carson snicker, and I knew it was officially time for us to go. "Okay." I stood, forcing her to lean back slightly, and she looked up at me. "It's time to head home."

"But things are just now getting fun."

"Frankie," I groaned.

"Olly." She repeated my name in the same tone I had just said hers, and I couldn't help but smile. She was too damn cute.

"Come on." I held my hand out to her, and she hesitated before finally slipping her fingers into mine with an eye roll.

"Fine, but just know that I didn't want to leave. You all are the ones who ended this party."

"It's noted." I laughed and looked over at Carson. "I'm taking her home. You need a ride?"

"No." He shook his head and smirked. "I'm good, but be careful with that one."

"I will be."

Frankie said bye to every single person we came across as

we left the party, and I was pretty sure that she didn't know half of their names. I tugged her along as she gave out hugs and air-kisses, and she was a giggling mess by the time we made it to my car.

"I'm coming." She laughed and leaned against the top of the door I had just opened for her. "Don't you ever just want to have a little fun?"

"I had plenty of fun tonight."

She rolled her eyes before sliding into the seat. "You spent more time brooding then having fun. You always do."

I closed the door behind her and moved to the driver's side without answering her. I did have fun tonight. I just couldn't seem to relax when she was around. Especially not with that many people and after everything that had happened.

And definitely not when she had been drinking.

I climbed into my seat and started the engine before looking at her. She had her head turned against the headrest and she was looking at me with the most satisfied look on her face.

"Are you okay?" I lifted my hand and placed it behind her as I backed out of the driveway.

"Never better."

I searched her eyes before putting the car in drive and pulling away from the party.

"You confuse me."

"Welcome to the club." She giggled and shifted in her seat.

"A few minutes ago you were complaining about me ruining your night by making you leave."

"This is true, but even though I have to go home, I now have the memory of you kissing me for the spank bank."

I almost ran off the road at her words. Frankie had never been so bold with the way she was speaking to me. "Jesus Christ, Frankie."

"What?" She shrugged her shoulders and relaxed into my passenger seat. "Would you prefer that I was thinking about someone else or that I get someone else to help me?"

I knew how I should have answered her. I should have told her yes. I should have broken this damn thing between us before we really fucked it up and sent her off to be happy with anyone else. But I couldn't get the damn word to leave my lips. No matter how hard I tried.

"I didn't think so." She chuckled softly, and I looked over just in time to see her run her hand down her neck and over her t-shirt. Her fingers pressed against her breast before it snaked even lower.

"What are you doing?" When she didn't answer me, I glanced back in her direction. "What the hell has gotten into you?"

"Just drive." She sighed. "Nothing has gotten into me. I'm just tired of being the perfect timid girl you all expect me to be." I heard the popping of her jeans button before the loud zipper filled the tight space.

"Fuck, Frankie." I looked over at her before quickly looking back at the road, but I saw her blue fingernails dipping below the edge of her jeans. "Stop."

"I'm not doing anything wrong." She was looking over at me again, and the feel of her, the smell of her, along with the smallest moan that passed her lips was almost my undoing. "Do you ever think of me when you touch yourself, Olly?"

I was so fucking hard against my jeans that it was becoming painful, but this wasn't right. This was crossing a line we couldn't come back from.

"You know I can't answer that."

"I like to imagine that you do." She whimpered as her hands began to move faster beneath her jeans. "I like to pretend that you want me just as badly as I want you. That when your cock is in your hand, you like to imagine that it's mine instead."

I pulled over on the side of the road before I wrecked my damn car and stared at her. She didn't stop her movements, not even for a second, and I knew that she wouldn't stop this unless I forced her to.

And I was no longer capable.

My voice shook as I spoke my next words. "We can't do this."

"We aren't doing anything." She blinked before biting down on her bottom lip. "I'm fingering myself."

"Fuck." Her hand moved beneath the fabric of her jeans, and I could practically imagine exactly what those fingers looked like sliding through her pussy. "Are you wet?"

She whimpered and brought her other hand up to knead her breast. "I'm so fucking wet, Olly."

I pressed my head back against my headrest and tried to control myself as I watched her. I had never seen her look more beautiful than she did right now, and every part of me was screaming for me to touch her.

I wanted to taste, bite, and fuck every inch of her body.

"Show me." She looked down at my cock before running her pink tongue over her bottom lip. "Show me what you do when you think about me."

"Frankie."

"No one is here." Her hand was still moving in tiny little circles, and they moved more rapidly the more she spoke.

"You can't possibly be doing anything wrong if you're only touching yourself. I just want to watch."

Her words were like a fucking drug, and I couldn't resist their pull.

"Please, Olly. I don't want my only experience to be with him."

My chest felt like it was going to crack open as her eyes pleaded with me. There was no chance in hell that I was going to deny her. There was no fucking way that I would be able to tell her no after what she just said.

I reached out and pushed her hair over her left shoulder so I got a clearer view of her face, then I tried not to overthink things as I slowly undid my belt and popped the button on my jeans.

She was watching my every move as if it pushed her further and further, and I thought I was going to come in my hand as I pulled my cock out of my pants and listened to her whimper.

"Oh God." She closed her eyes and slammed her head back against the headrest as I began to move my hand. Her thighs were trembling beneath her touch, and I was desperate to feel that vibration against my tongue. I wanted to know every little movement of her body.

But more than anything, I was desperate to erase anyone from her memory but me.

"Tell me what you want." I barely recognized my voice as I spoke, but I was too far gone to worry about it.

"You." Her answer was instant. "I wish it was your hand touching me. I wish you were the one making me come."

I squeezed the tip of my cock in my fist and closed my eyes.

"I wish your mouth was on me. I wish I could taste you. I've never..."

I leaned across the seat and jerked her hand from her jeans. There was an instant mark of shock and anger across her face, but it disappeared the moment I brought her fingers to my mouth and slid them along my tongue.

She tasted better than I could imagine, and my hand moved faster as her wetness spread throughout my mouth.

"You taste so fucking good." I kissed the tip of her fingers, and she watched me, mesmerized.

"I want to taste you."

"Not tonight." I shook my head.

"Please," she begged me, and I almost caved. I would have given just about anything to watch my cock disappear between her lips. I knew how soft her tongue was from the kiss earlier, and I could imagine how lethal it would be against my cock.

I reached across the seat and wrapped my hands around her. It took nothing to lift her to me, and she settled against me with her back pressed against my chest and her chest pressed to the steering wheel.

My cock was settled between her thighs, and I could feel the heat of her through her jeans. She moved her hips against me, as desperate to feel me as I was to feel her.

"Olly," she moaned my name and pressed her head back against my shoulder before turning her face to meet mine.

I didn't allow myself to think as I kissed her. I just took what I had been wanting for so damn long. She kissed me back with just as much want. We were a clash of lips and teeth, and I nipped at her bottom lip as I allowed my hand to press against her stomach. I could feel her trembling beneath my touch.

I circled her belly button with my middle finger, and she sucked in a harsh breath. I didn't hesitate as I slid my hand lower and pushed my fingers beneath her jeans. I was met with how wet she was almost instantly, and I bit down on her shoulder as I thrust my hips forward.

She was soft, so damn soft, and so fucking wet. I pushed my fingers through her pussy and swirled her wetness around as I went.

"Please, Olly."

I pushed my fingers down against her clit and her loud moan filled my car. I didn't give her time to adjust to the feeling. I began to move against her clit, my hand as harsh as my hips beneath her. I was forcing her body down against mine, and she began to move against me with the same roughness.

"You have no idea how long I've wanted to do this." I lifted my left hand to her neck and used my thumb to force her face to mine. I sucked her bottom lip into my mouth before kissing her, hard. "I've thought about how fucking good your pussy would feel every day. I've never felt anything better."

She moaned against my mouth, and I moved my hand farther down and sank my middle two fingers into her. She started riding my hand as I pumped in and out of her and pressed the heel of my palm into her clit.

"I want you to fuck me." She ran her lips along mine.

Her words shocked me and tormented me. I buried my face in her neck as I moved my fingers faster inside of her. I wanted to fuck her more than I had ever wanted anything else, but I couldn't. Not tonight. Not like this.

Frankie deserved better.

She deserved better than I was giving her now, but there was no way I could stop.

"Not tonight." I shook my head and lapped at the skin of her neck. "Just let me give you this."

She didn't answer. She just began moving harder and faster against me, her body chasing the feeling I was giving her, and every move of her hips pushed me further and further to the edge.

My phone vibrated in my cupholder, the loud noise ringing out around us, but neither of us stopped. If anything, we chased the feeling of just the two of us even harder.

We were blocking out everything that existed outside of this moment, and God, it felt like a dream.

"I'm going to come, Olly." She pressed her head back against my shoulder, and I tightened my fingers on her throat. Her heart was hammering beneath my touch, and I matched my fingers to the rhythm as they pumped in and out of her.

I felt like we were racing, hunting a feeling that we had been desperately wanting from each other for far too long, and it was finally within our grasp. Her hands pushed into my thighs, her fingers digging into my jeans as she held on and rode me harder.

I was going to come, and she had barely even touched me.

She pressed her mouth to mine, and I kissed her. My fingers dug into her neck as my tongue caressed hers, and she cried out against my mouth as she tightened her thighs and her body tensed above me.

Her scream was muffled against my mouth as her orgasm raced through her, and I couldn't last another second. I came against her thighs and pressed my mouth down roughly against hers. I wasn't ready to give her up, to give up this feeling, so I kissed her until both of our breathing had calmed and my heart rate returned to some-what normal.

I ran my tongue over her bottom lip before slowly pulling away, and I searched her eyes as she stared at me. She looked so tired yet so damn blissful, and I knew I was looking at her the same way.

"Are you okay?" I asked just as the reality of what we had just done started to hit me.

Beck was going to kill me. He was going to hate me.

Frankie had been drinking, and she wasn't thinking clearly. I was a fucking idiot. I should have never allowed this to happen.

"I'm more than okay." She leaned forward and kissed me again. This one was slow and lazy and felt like she was trying to erase every thought that had just flooded me. "I've wanted this for so long."

"You've been drinking."

She raised her hand and pressed it against my mouth before I could continue. "Stop," she whispered against her hand. "Please give me at least a few minutes before you ruin this."

I tried to listen to what she was saying, but my mind was still racing with the thought that I should have regretted what we had just done. But I didn't.

Not even a little bit.

Even though I tried to force the feeling to come.

I knew that I should have. I should have been freaking out and demanding that Frankie get off me, but the feel of her against me was far too good. This felt like it was exactly where she was meant to be.

And even as my heart raced with the thought of what Beck would do, I didn't regret her.

"Do you have to go home now?" she murmured against her now slack fingers as she pressed her forehead against mine.

"We should," I whispered before kissing her fingertips that were still pressed against my mouth.

"I don't want to," she whispered back so quietly that I almost didn't hear her.

"I know. Me either." I gripped her jaw in my hand and brought her mouth back to mine. I kissed her until I was hard beneath her again.

"Let's get you home." I pressed a kiss to her forehead even as the dread of leaving this moment settled in my chest, and she nodded against my mouth.

THANK YOU

Thank you so much for reading Allie and Carson's story!

This story meant so much to me, and I hope you loved it as much as I do!

Frankie and Olly's story begins in The Seduction of Pretty Lies. Continue reading for a sneak peak at their story.

I would love for you to join my reader group, Hollywood, so we can connect and talk about all of your The Taste of an Enemy thoughts. This group is the first place to find out about cover reveals, book news, and new releases!

Again, thank you for going on this wild journey with me.

Xo,
Holly Renee
www.authorhollyrenee.com

Before You Go
Please consider leaving an honest review.